"Please be careful," Charlie warned her

"If you think we need to get out of this Blackwater Lake project, you have my blessing. Money isn't everything," he said.

"I know. If things get dicey, I'll ditch it." Although that might be easier said than done. "And don't worry about Zack Maynard," Liza added. "I'll be so helpful he'll be ready to go back to San Francisco, just like that." She snapped her fingers.

"Believe it or not, Zack's really a nice guy."

"He's sure a handsome devil, I'll give him that much. The nice part is debatable."

"Is that right? You think I'm good-looking?"

There was no doubt about the owner of that rich baritone. Darn! If only the floor would open up and swallow her. Somehow the subject of their conversation had shown up in the restaurant and was now standing next to their table in all his handsomeness.

Charlie didn't miss a beat as he stood to shake Zack's hand. "Sit down. I want to formally introduce you to my friend, my business partner and your project manager—Liza Henderson."

Dear Reader,

Welcome back to Magnolia Bluffs, Georgia, where Liza Henderson and her buddies are up to their hoopskirts in murder and mayhem. Liza leads a busy life keeping up with her wild and wacky family while running a successful architecture/planning firm. Zack Maynard is a San Francisco homicide detective. He's in Georgia investigating vandalism at the family-owned real estate development project that Liza manages. The job was supposed to be a piece of cake, but he quickly discovers that beneath the slow and easy Georgia facade there's a nest of felons. It doesn't take long for Liza and Zack to find themselves on a collision course with some *nasty* folks.

Like most star-crossed lovers, they have more baggage than a Samsonite store. Meaningful relationships— are you kidding? But in the end they realize there's a time and place to risk everything for the greatest reward of all—true love. And it's especially sweet the second time around.

Ann

P.S. I love hearing from my readers. My mailing address is P.O. Box 97313, Tacoma, WA 98497, and my e-mail address is ann@ann-defee.com. Please write!

Goin' Down to Georgia
Ann DeFee

TORONTO • NEW YORK • LONDON
AMSTERDAM • PARIS • SYDNEY • HAMBURG
STOCKHOLM • ATHENS • TOKYO • MILAN • MADRID
PRAGUE • WARSAW • BUDAPEST • AUCKLAND

ISBN-13: 978-0-373-75206-5
ISBN-10:   0-373-75206-7

GOIN' DOWN TO GEORGIA

This edition published by arrangement with Harlequin Books S.A.

® and TM are trademarks of the publisher. Trademarks indicated with ® are registered in the United States Patent and Trademark Office, the Canadian Trade Marks Office and in other countries.

www.eHarlequin.com

Printed in U.S.A.

ABOUT THE AUTHOR

Ann DeFee's debut novel, *A Texas State of Mind* (Harlequin American Romance), was a double finalist in the 2006 Romance Writers of America's prestigious RITA® Awards.

Drawing on her background as a fifth-generation Texan, Ann loves to take her readers into the sassy and sometimes wacky world of a small Southern community. As an air force wife with twenty-three moves under her belt, she's now settled in her tree house in the Pacific Northwest with her husband, their golden retriever and two very spoiled cats. When she's not writing, you can probably find her on the tennis court or in the park with her walking group.

She loves to hear from her readers, so please visit her Web site at www.ann-defee.com. Or contact her by snail mail at P.O. Box 97313, Tacoma, WA 98497.

Books by Ann DeFee

HARLEQUIN AMERICAN ROMANCE
1076—A TEXAS STATE OF MIND
1115—TEXAS BORN
1155—SOMEWHERE DOWN IN TEXAS
1176—GEORGIA ON HIS MIND

HARLEQUIN EVERLASTING LOVE
16—SUMMER AFTER SUMMER

To my beautiful grandbabies—
Scotty, Emily, Caitlyn and Juliet

And a special thanks to the Fates that pushed,
prodded and shoved me in the right direction.
You guys rock!

Chapter One

"No!" Liza Henderson's life flashed before her eyes as she prepared to meet her maker.

"Damn! Damn! Damn!" Screeching expletives probably wasn't a good way to make it through the pearly gates, but hey, she was about to get flattened by a tire careening off a chicken hauler.

Liza gripped the wheel of her ancient F-250. Lurching off the road, she bounced across a gravel verge and came to rest in a tangle of kudzu vines.

She felt as if time hiccuped when the chicken hauler—sans one tire—sideswiped a truck pulling a double-wide trailer, sending both vehicles sliding, blocking the westbound lanes. That was bad enough, but the comedy of errors wasn't quite over. When a molasses truck joined the melee, it turned into a sticky wicket.

Not only had State Highway 441 north of Magnolia Bluffs, Georgia, been transformed into a gooey, feathery chicken hell, the three truck drivers had abandoned their mangled rigs and were about to come to blows.

The good news was that no one appeared to be hurt. The bad news was that Liza was trapped in a sea of greenery.

She was prying her fingers from the steering wheel when a state trooper tapped on the passenger-side window.

"Ma'am, are you okay?"

If Liza discounted the fact that her heart was trying to beat its way out of her chest, she supposed she was just dandy. She scooted over to roll down the window, mentally taking inventory of her body parts.

"I think so. Everything seems to be in working order."

"That's good. I'll mosey over there and see if I can round up some guys to help you get back on the road." The trooper indicated the long line of cars and pickups that had stacked up on the highway.

"Ya know, if you sit too long in that kudzu, it'll cover you right up," he said with a grin. "If that happens, they'll never find you."

Imported from Japan in the nineteenth century and used during the Depression for erosion control, kudzu was capable of growing almost a foot a day. It also had the annoying habit of covering everything in its way—up to and including derelict cars, sheds, abandoned washing machines and, on occasion, a slow-moving granny.

"Amen to that," Liza agreed. Everyone knew about the scourge of the South.

The trooper stepped back and did a double take when he glanced in the bed of her pickup. "Ma'am, not to be nosy, but is that a purple bathtub you have back there?"

"Unfortunately it is." Not to mention a sink and a toilet.

"I've never seen anything quite like it before. Didn't realize they made 'em that color."

Neither had Liza. Not until her daughter Cassie had conned her into returning the fixtures to the Designer's Mart in Atlanta.

The trooper shook his head in a "what next" gesture. "Let me go get some fellas to help ya."

True to his word, the patrolman returned with a crew of able-bodied men—ready, willing and able to extricate Liza's Ford from the all-consuming vegetation. It took some grunting, cussing and a few snickers before the gang of good old boys managed to get her back on the road.

Liza breathed a sigh of relief. At least she hadn't been whooshed off to the white light, but still, this was turning out to be a day straight out of Dante's Inferno. It had started with a predawn call from Kara, her youngest. Since Kara had left for her freshman year at Emory University, her communication skills had deteriorated, so a phone call before dawn was not a good sign.

Liza loved her daughter like crazy, but Kara *was* a drama queen. Normally that wasn't a problem. This time, however, her college tuition and rent were due, *and* she'd maxed out her credit card at a Rich's department-store sale.

Step one—discuss fiscal responsibility. Step two—assure her hysterical daughter that money was forthcoming. Step three—ask what Rich's had in size-six shoes. And step four—hang up and reach for the bottle of aspirin and a cup of coffee. That had helped until her other daughter, Cassie, called.

An incredibly mature twenty-three-year-old, Cassie had married a widowed dentist with two sons, Josh and Jason, ages seven and eight. It didn't seem to bother Cassie that Jim McGuire was almost twelve years her senior—they were madly in love. And what more could Liza want for her daughter? So almost overnight, Cassie had assumed the role of mom and Liza had acquired a new name—Grammy.

The girl could sell plasma TVs to nomads, so Liza had given in to the inevitable. She'd reluctantly agreed to return the aubergine—a fancy word for *purple*—toilet. Was she a sucker, or what? Of course—she was a mom.

The longer Liza sat in the traffic jam, the crankier she became. It was foggy. It was hot. It was humid. And to make matters worse, she had a raging case of PMS.

Get a grip! In a situation like this, her best option was to loosen up with a Tim McGraw CD, a bag of Cheetos and an RC Cola. Her mama didn't think Cheetos and an RC were a proper snack for a lady, but then, she'd also rather die than wear white shoes after Labor Day. And as for having a *daughter* who wore a hard hat to work—needless to say, that was a subject to be avoided.

Liza slipped off her sandals, planted her feet on the dash and contemplated her near-death experience. She'd been cooling her heels for almost an hour when some guy in a beer truck started making eyes at her. The postpubescent lech would have diddled his drawers if he'd realized he was making kissy faces at a forty-four-year-old *grandmother.* Technically, she was a stepgrandma, but that was irrelevant.

When he pressed his face to the glass for another round of wet, blubbery lips, Liza decided it was time to give him a one-fingered salute. She'd just folded her hand in the proper fist when her cell phone chirped. Bubba had been saved by the bell.

"This is Liza."

"How's my best girl?" The voice was male, familiar and most certainly trouble.

"Nope," she said, although she'd never been able to say no to Charlie Taylor and mean it. He was her business partner and one of her oldest friends. During the darkest period of Liza's life, he'd been her rock. "Whatever it is, forget it," she teased.

"Why do you think I want something?"

"Because I have your number. Remember, I've known you since you were blowing milk out your nose in junior high."

Charlie laughed. "I suppose I'll never live that down." He paused before getting to the nitty-gritty. "We have a problem, and I need you to do me a favor."

Liza sighed, knowing she'd capitulate. "Give me the details. But if it has to be accomplished in the next hour or two, you're out of luck."

"Where are you?"

"I'm on 441 in a terrible traffic jam."

Charlie burst into laughter. "They've been talking about that on the radio."

"Stuff it, Taylor. What's the deal?"

When he cleared his throat, Liza knew it was bad.

"I hate to tell you this, but I just heard from Zack Maynard. He'll be here in a couple of hours."

Damn it! Norton Development, a California company, had purchased a huge tract of land on which to build an upscale community appealing to Atlanta commuters. Savvy businessmen that they were, they realized a local presence was necessary, so they'd contracted Taylor and Henderson Land Planning Consultants to manage the project.

"Are you kidding?" Of course he wasn't. For months, the Norton head honcho had been threatening to sic Zack Maynard on them. Sure, they'd had some accidents—okay, a shooting— on the job site. That didn't mean Liza needed a buttinski investigator looking over her shoulder.

"Nope, he's definitely on his way. According to my voice mail, his plane was diverted to Birmingham because of fog. He had to take a bus from there to Atlanta." Charlie didn't bother to conceal his chuckle. "He tried to rent a car, but there wasn't anything available, so he's coming in on another coach."

"Buses?" Liza almost choked on her cola. "Mr. Hotshot is taking buses?"

Ever the diplomat, Charlie ignored her. "I was planning to pick him up, but I've had an emergency."

Understanding finally dawned. "No way!"

"Come on," he cajoled. "You'll have to meet him eventually. I'll betcha he looks around, gets bored and heads back to San Francisco."

"What part of 'no' don't you understand? You promised you'd deal with him if he showed up. What happened to that?"

"Liza, sweetie, I wouldn't ask unless I was in a real bind."

Despite being irritated with Charlie, Liza couldn't suppress a giggle. "I'll bet he's not a happy camper."

"You're probably right. But you can charm him, I know you can."

"Flattery won't get you anywhere." Talk about a big fat lie.

"Let me tell you about a couple of negatives with this scenario," Liza said. "For one thing, I have Cassie's bathroom fixtures in the back of my truck. *And* I'm not exactly dressed for business. I'm wearing a ratty pair of shorts and a T-shirt. All I need to pull off the *Grapes of Wrath* look is a mattress and some livestock." Liza giggled again. "We have plenty of fowl out here, but I'm not about to grab a couple of them." She either had to go with levity or resort to profanity.

"Maynard is not going to be impressed," she said.

"My only other choice is Yvonne, and she hasn't renewed her driver's license."

Liza sighed. "All right, all right. I'll pick him up, but you owe me."

"You're a sweetheart. I'll call him and let him know."

"Mr. Big's gonna have to wait until I can get out of this mess." Liza winced, glancing at the interior of her ancient pickup. "I hope he has a sense of humor. This has all the makings of an Ellie Mae Clampett moment."

"He works for a real-estate developer. I'm sure he's seen it all." Charlie laughed at his own wit. "You're a real sport. And I'm dying of curiosity. What are you doing with bathroom fixtures in your truck?"

"Cassie's redecorating, and after she bought this stuff she decided it wasn't in tune with her aura," Liza said. "Against my better judgment I agreed to return it."

"Let me get this straight." Liza could picture him smacking his head. "My dingbat goddaughter thinks she has to coordinate her toilet with her aura?"

"Yep," Liza said. "And seeing how you've always indulged her, it's partly your fault. By the way, what's your emergency?" She figured he had some unexpected problem on a construction site, or a public hearing that had been changed.

There was a pause, and when he spoke his voice assumed a sober quality she'd never heard from Charlie before.

"It has to do with the murders."

"The murders!" she squeaked.

The talk of the county was the abduction and murder of several people involved in the real-estate industry. Most people suspected environmentalists protesting recent development were behind it, although no one had claimed responsibility. Regardless of the motivation, the crime wave had sent everyone skittering for cover.

"I got a threatening letter," Charlie said. "It rambled on about how I had to pay for past misdeeds. Jeez! I'm a nice guy—what have I done to make someone that mad?"

"Do you suppose it could be a sick joke?" Liza knew that wasn't the case, but she had to ask.

"Your uncle Dave doesn't think so." Uncle Dave was also known as Sheriff Dave Madison. "He's coming by to talk to me. That's why I can't pick up Maynard. But I'm going to be optimistic and assume it's a prank."

From the tone of his voice, Liza knew Charlie didn't believe that any more than she did, but she'd play along. "Sure, it's probably a practical joke."

"Call me when traffic loosens up. In the meantime, I'll make sure Maynard knows we haven't forgotten him. After you pick him up, why don't you bring him to the office? That way I can meet him. Besides, I'm dying to see the bathtub."

"You're pushing your luck, Taylor."

He responded with another laugh.

It took another hour for the troopers to divert traffic around the accident. If Liza hurried, she might be able to beat Mr. Maynard's bus. If not, he could sit and wait.

No skin off her nose.

Chapter Two

Zack Maynard stared out the dingy bus window at the thick white fog that drifted and curled around the fuel pumps of the combination gas station/convenience store. The pungent odor of diesel hung in the humid air. The lying jerk at the airport had claimed it would be an easy hour's jaunt from Atlanta to Magnolia Bluffs. That guy needed his butt kicked up and down the tarmac.

Zack felt as if he'd been on the road for at least a decade, but in reality he'd only been stuck in the alternate universe of planes and buses for eighteen hours. Unfortunately, he was now trapped in the vehicle from hell with crabby tourists, crying babies and disgruntled businessmen. He hadn't eaten in hours, and it didn't take a pit check to realize he was getting ripe. In other words— he was whipped, beaten, exhausted and downright grumpy.

He needed caffeine, food and a bathroom with a flush toilet— and not necessarily in that order. In desperation, he wandered into Tommy Gene's grocery store/bait shop and auto repair. On a "dump" scale of one to ten, this place rated an eleven. But at least the bathroom wasn't an outhouse, and the coffee was black, syrupy and hot. Now, if he could find something that wouldn't poison him, he'd have it made.

The burritos had an uncanny resemblance to petrified ostrich eggs. Even a cop on a stakeout wouldn't eat those things, and the greasy fried chicken… He'd pass, thank you very much. He picked up some Twinkies, a bag of Doritos and a supersize coffee instead.

Zack was fantasizing about a shower, a toothbrush, a hot meal and a soft bed as he made his way down the grimy aisle of the bus and threw his sack on the empty seat. As he caught sight of his reflection in the window, he realized he could have passed for someone on *America's Most Wanted*.

He sat down on the grubby velour and tore open the Twinkies. Penny would appreciate his dilemma. Although outwardly prim and proper, Penny was a dynamo who'd worked for the family business more years than Zack could remember. And speaking of Penny, it was time to check in with his mother hen. He punched the speed dial on his cell phone.

"Hey, Penny, my love, what's happening?"

"Don't 'what's happening' me, you donkey's butt," she exploded. "I've been worried sick about you. I put you on a plane ages ago, and you up and disappeared. I knew you didn't make it to Podunk, Georgia, like you were supposed to, but did you call and tell me where you were? Noooo! You let me worry. So don't get all cheerful with me now."

"I'm fine, and how are you?" He didn't dare laugh.

"I want a complete rundown of what's happened and where you are."

Zack scrubbed his face with his hand. "About ten minutes after we took off, a flight attendant dumped a cup of coffee in my lap." He grimaced, recalling the painful incident.

Penny had the audacity to snicker. "Go on, I'm listening."

"It wasn't funny. I'm lucky I can still walk. Then some perky kid disguised as an airline employee informed us that Hartsfield airport was fogged in so they sent us to Birmingham. We sat in the airport and waited and waited and waited for the weather to clear. I thought I'd go nuts."

"And…"

He ran his hand down the stubble on his face. "The fog never lifted, so they put us on a bus. When I got to Atlanta, the car-rental agency had no record of my reservation, and everything from a Mini to a Hummer was already booked. Now I'm on another Greyhound, and fed up with this B.S." Zack glanced at his crumpled suit jacket. "And I smell like a pair of dirty gym socks."

"I can't believe it!" Penny howled with laughter. "Mr. Handsome-as-sin police detective has turned into a bum. I'd pay a bundle to see that." When she could finally control herself, she asked, "So now what?"

"Keep laughing and I'll have Kevin fire you. I'm not a silent partner in the business for nothing," he said. Although Zack's dad had divided Norton Development equally, his half brother, Kevin, actually ran the business. That was great, since Zack's first love was law enforcement.

"We're making a potty stop, and I'm doing some five-star dining on a Twinkie."

Penny's raucous laughter came through loud and clear.

"I'm hoping we get to Magnolia Bluffs before noon, but who knows? I called Charlie Taylor to make sure someone will be there to pick me up."

"Since there's nothing I can do for you, do you want me to tell your brother you called?"

"Yeah, he'll get a kick out of this. Tell him I'll be in touch tomorrow." Zack clicked off and leaned back to contemplate his situation.

This was one heck of a bad patch! And not just today, either. At thirty-nine, he was too young for a midlife crisis. However, he'd already had his own version of the red Corvette and blond bimbo with a slight variation on the old cliché. His red Corvette was a black Porsche; the blond bimbo was his leggy, voluptuous ex-wife, Angela. Unfortunately, the honeymoon euphoria had barely worn off when he'd discovered she was more interested in his portfolio than in him.

Angela's addiction to shopping was bad enough, but he could overlook that flaw. What he couldn't forgive was the affair she'd had with her old college boyfriend—so much for marital bliss and the till-death-do-us-part vow.

Lately she'd been showing up uninvited at his apartment. It almost felt as if she was stalking him. But the final straw was when she moved some of her clothes into his closet while he was at work. The woman was delusional if she thought he'd take her back. No way, no how!

She'd always been stubborn, but this time she'd gone too far. Zack was more than willing to give her money, but it was becoming increasingly obvious that Angela's goal was to resume her status as Mrs. Zack Maynard.

And regrettably, his ex wasn't his primary headache. When his captain had wimped out and put him on indefinite administrative leave from the San Francisco Police Department, Zack had been tempted to dig himself a hole and jump in. Instead, he'd let Kevin talk him into this cockamamie trip to Georgia. The hole was looking better and better all the time.

Zack was mulling over his problems with Angela, his captain's lack of a backbone and the favor he was doing for Kevin when a young boy raced down the aisle with an ice cream cone clutched in his fist. Sure enough, the kid tripped and smeared cold, melting chocolate all the way down the front of Zack's shirt. Jeez, Louise! The mess ran in rivulets toward the waistband of his khakis.

He desperately wanted to beat his head against the window, but considering how his luck was going, he'd probably end up with cooties.

Chapter Three

This day was getting better and better. Liza stood in front of the Magnolia Inn—aka the bus station—clutching a sign she'd scribbled on a loose page of Josh's homework. She was parked in a loading zone and Deputy Booty Carter was lurking around, itching to ticket her. If this Maynard guy was smart, he'd take one look at her 1983 pickup and beat feet back to the bus.

Mama always said confidence could conquer anything. Liza scowled. That was great advice coming from a woman who wore pearls to the Piggly Wiggly. Liza might look like Ellie Mae, but she was a respected member of the business community. Heck, she even had a law degree.

So instead of hyperventilating, Liza visualized her favorite power suit and very high heels. Considering she was barely five feet tall, she needed all the help she could get. Forget the shorts and T-shirt; she'd radiate self-assurance and professionalism. Sure—right after she sold him the Brooklyn Bridge.

Liza watched as the second bus of the morning rumbled up to the overhang, disgorging its passengers. She held up her homemade poster, hoping Maynard would see it.

The first passengers were either the wrong age or the wrong gender. A young mother grabbed a fussy toddler before the child could catapult out the door. A couple of teens with gym bags and backward baseball hats elbowed each other as they ambled down the steps. Her best bet was the middle-aged man in a suit. He was eliminated when he broke into a smile and waved at a woman on the other end of the sidewalk.

Distracted momentarily by a honking horn, Liza spun back around just in time to glimpse a rumpled, absolutely gorgeous guy emerging from the bus. He was wrestling with his laptop and a bulky carry-on, and—as her fraternal twin Maizie would say— *woo, woo, woo!*

Too bad he wasn't her boy. Not only was he handsome, he was entirely too athletic-looking to be some two-bit wannabe investigator. The guy was a devastating combo of Paul Newman's blue eyes, Mel Gibson's tush and George Clooney's smile. Though someone should probably tell him that Colombo was okay as a detective, but he was *not* a good fashion consultant.

An exuberant reunion at the bottom of the steps held up the remaining passengers and gave Liza a few more minutes to inspect him—late thirties with hints of silver in his dark hair, eyelashes to die for and a *don't mess with me* frown on his face.

Liza was still checking out his sexy buns when she heard a crash that sounded way too close to her truck. Merciful heavens! Some nitwit had knocked off her back bumper and was barreling off in a cloud of black, oily smoke.

She took off at a sprint. Maybe, just maybe, she could get a license-plate number.

"Stop! Stop!" she screeched. "You idiot! That's hit-and-run." Liza paused, gagging from the fumes.

She really wanted to pitch a fit, but somehow she controlled herself and merely slammed the bumper into the bed of the truck together with the purple bathtub. Fantastic! All she needed were some hubcaps and a minnow bucket and every redneck in town would be hitting on her.

"Please, please tell me that sign you're waving around doesn't say Maynard." Mr. Handsome was glaring at her as if she was decked out in full hillbilly regalia. The man probably thought he'd stepped into *The Twilight Zone*.

Liza was absolutely mortified. She waved the sign, trying to stifle her coughing. "Are you Maynard? I'm Liza."

The man's lip twitched as if he was trying to hide a grin. He had the most gorgeous dimples and he was laughing at her! How dare he chortle when she wanted to expire from embarrassment?

"Yeah, I'm Zack Maynard."

There went the dimples again. No doubt about it, he thought she was a rube. Before Liza could reply, he wandered toward the pile of luggage on the sidewalk. Well, didn't that just take the cake. The first guy in forever to get her juices flowing, and he dismissed her as an Appalachian bimbo. She'd admit she wasn't dressed for a board meeting, but that didn't give him the right to laugh at her.

She should count to ten, take a deep breath and remain calm. She could do it. She knew she could. Unfortunately, she hadn't counted on the power of a bruised ego.

Mama said that even a fish wouldn't get in trouble if it kept its mouth shut. Too bad Liza always managed to forget that. She snatched the handle of the suitcase. "Guess what, buddy, you're not in San Francisco anymore. You're in the South. And we have some unwritten rules here. People are polite and civilized, even if they're grumpy. We say 'yes, sir' and 'no, sir.'" Her voice rose as she waved her hands in the air. "We smile at clerks. We honk only if we're about to hit someone. We don't jaywalk. We talk to people in elevators. And most important, we don't laugh at strangers. Now give me that suitcase, and let's get out of here."

ZACK WAS DEAD ON HIS FEET, but he was still smart enough to realize he'd seriously irritated the little elf trying to yank the suitcase out of his hands. Although the woman looked vaguely like Winona Ryder, her glare was vintage Joan Crawford. What in the world was she talking about—jaywalking, elevators, store clerks?

"Madam, please let go of my suitcase. I saw your sign." He indicated the piece of notebook paper she was still holding. "And I mistakenly thought you'd been sent to pick me up." He enunciated every word like he was speaking to a not-too-bright three-year-old.

The elf went up on her tiptoes, but still couldn't get nose to nose with him. "I *am* here to pick you up. Let go of the stupid suitcase and we'll leave."

Zack had heard Southerners could be squirrelly, but this one beat all. He was too busy wondering if she was planning to smack him to notice that a policeman had ambled up.

"Is there a problem here?" the cop drawled.

A cop with a gut and a gun—hmm. Sanity returned with a vengeance. Zack dropped the piece of luggage. "No problem. We were just discussing who'd carry the bag, and my little friend wants the pleasure. So I'll let her."

He turned to Liza, who was till twitching with anger. "Grab the stuff and let's get going," he instructed, handing her his carry-on.

Not one to leave well enough alone, he volleyed another shot. "Be careful, I don't want anything broken." He turned quickly so she wouldn't see his grin, but he heard her growl. She actually snarled at him. How about that?

"Is that *pickup* your vehicle?" he asked.

He didn't need eyes in the back of his head to realize she was giving him another deadly glare. She'd grabbed the two suitcases and was trying to keep up with his long-legged stride. He'd award her an A+ for determination.

"Maynard, wait up," she panted. "What do you have in here, bricks?" she groused, lugging the heavy suitcase down the sidewalk.

Zack debated whether to tell her it had wheels. That *would* be the gentlemanly thing to do, but the devil on his shoulder won out. This woman was incredibly entertaining, and in the past day and a half, he hadn't had too many chuckles.

Zack strolled leisurely toward the rattletrap. When he looked back, he noticed she'd discovered the wheels and was making better time, but her mood hadn't improved. She was a beauty even if she was stomping along like a pint-size Godzilla in a snit.

When they got closer to the Bondo-mobile, Zack spied her cargo and almost hooted. Kevin would die if he could see how far down the ladder they rated.

"Okay," he said with a grin. "I've been a good sport so far. What are you, a junk dealer or a deranged pixie? And why do you have a purple bathroom in your truck?"

"Aubergine," she said, gazing intently at the pavement.

"What's an aubergine?" He ran his fingers through his hair. "It sounds like an overripe avocado."

"Aubergine, you Neanderthal, is an eggplant. Purple!" she shouted. "And I'm not a pixie, I'm a *grandmother*."

Holding up his hands in mock surrender, Zack backed off. He could play this game. "If we don't want the cop to come back, we'd better throw my bags in the truck and get out of here." He ambled over to the passenger-side door. Hiding a smile, he watched as she struggled to stow the luggage. Finally, she gave up and dumped the carry-on bag in the bathtub.

She slammed the tailgate shut before marching to the driver's side and jumping in. It was obvious she wanted to leave him standing in the road, since she only grudgingly unlocked his door. But she barely allowed him time to get in before she shoved the truck into gear.

Zack clutched the scuffed plastic armrest as they zoomed into traffic. He leaned his head back against the seat. This whole trip had been a long free fall down Alice's rabbit hole. He half expected to see a hare, complete with waistcoat and monocle, thumbing a ride.

Chapter Four

The silence in the pickup was as comfortable as a toxic-waste dump. Liza felt like a first-class idiot. Mr. Way-Too-Sexy investigator should shuffle back to San Francisco. Then she could have a private little nervous breakdown. Her current insanity had to be the result of a hormonal surge.

Liza took a deep breath. In truth, he hadn't done a thing to warrant her shrewish behavior. The problem was she felt humiliated. Everyone in town said she was the only one in her family with a lick of common sense, so she'd better start using it.

Then Liza came up with a plan. She'd deliver Mr. Maynard and his luggage to Charlie's office. After that she could go straight home for a glass of wine and a soak in the hot tub. By gosh, she was a professional.

Liza suppressed a sigh. What had gotten into her? She'd had a screaming match with a client at the bus station. And Lord knows, ladies don't scream in public places. But she'd done that and more. It was a miracle Booty Carter hadn't hauled them in for disorderly conduct. Ever since she'd turned him down for the Rotary dance, he'd been out to get her.

And Mama would positively die if she'd had to post bail. The key here was to act cool and professional.

Their offices were in a restored antebellum home near the town square. Liza pulled in behind the building and stopped under one of the gorgeous magnolias that dotted the property. She pulled on the parking brake and reached across Maynard's lap to fiddle with the tricky door handle. Bad idea! It took only a microsecond to realize she'd made a huge mistake. She looked up into crystalline blue eyes that were flecked with hints of green.

"The person at the front desk is Yvonne. Tell Charlie I have an errand to run and I'll be back in a couple of minutes."

ZACK'S GRIN GOT WIDER. Although he was sure she'd gladly slit his throat, he couldn't resist teasing her.

He jumped from the truck, looked her over and mimicked his idea of a prep-school snob. "You're bringing in the suitcases, aren't you?" In response to his taunt, she threw the truck into gear and pulled away, barely missing his toes.

"Don't scratch the leather—it's Italian," he yelled as the truck disappeared in a spray of gravel. He definitely needed to restrain his evil gremlin—the one who was trying to get him killed.

Reverting to his cop persona, Zack checked out his surroundings. Taylor and Henderson's office was Tara revisited, complete with honeysuckle, ferns, white wicker furniture and a big yellow cat.

Zack paused in front of the massive doors. This trip wasn't his idea, but Kevin's trouble-meter was hardly ever wrong.

He approached the blonde behind an antique desk. "You must be Yvonne. I'm Zack Maynard. Mr. Taylor's expecting me."

"Yes, he is. Where's Liza, uh, Mrs. Henderson?" The woman peered around him.

So his chauffeur was married to Henderson, the project manager. Too bad. But he wasn't looking for any kind of companionship; this was a business trip, nothing more.

"If you mean the woman who picked me up, she said she had an errand to run and she'd be right back." He laughed, thinking about their encounter. "With the way that lunatic drives, who knows?"

The receptionist frowned as she reached for the phone.

"Charlie, Mr. Maynard is here and Liza's coming, I guess." She turned to Zack. "Down the hall, first door on the left. Did you leave your luggage in the car?"

"Yep, she's bringing it in."

"*Liza's* bringin' your suitcase in?"

"Yes, ma'am." Zack felt like a kid again. He hadn't said *ma'am* in twenty years. It probably had something to do with the mint-julep atmosphere.

A tall man with a big grin sauntered down the hall. "I'm Charlie Taylor," he said. "Let's go back to my office. You look like you could use a drink."

As a matter of fact, Zack would've paid big bucks for a good cup of coffee. "Sounds great." He followed his host, hoping he'd find one at the end of the plush carpet. "I have a question. Do you always send Little Miss Sunshine to welcome your business associates? She drives like Dale Earnhardt Jr."

Charlie frowned. "I thought Liza was picking you up."

"Yep, that's her. She almost got us arrested at the bus station." Zack laughed at the incredulous expression on Charlie's face. "Not only that, she tried to run over my toes when she dropped me off. And God only knows where she took my luggage." He was about to continue when he heard a gasp behind him. Charlie's receptionist had joined them in the office and was staring at him as if he were a raving lunatic. Charlie was doing a bit of gawking himself.

The spell was broken by an irritated voice, or as irritated as a honeyed drawl could manage. "Charlie Taylor, you get out here. I have a major bone to pick with you."

Zack raised an eyebrow. "See what I mean?"

The three of them stepped into the hall to see what was happening.

"Why are you carrying that stuff?" Charlie asked. Liza was dragging two huge suitcases and had a carry-on perched precariously on one shoulder.

She dropped the bags and stabbed a finger at Charlie. "If you ever pull something like this again, you can consider our friendship canceled, your godfathership annulled and your good name besmirched. And you can tell that unctuous, punctilious, *supercilious* jerk I wouldn't work with him if he was the last client on earth and I was down to my final penny!"

With that parting shot, Liza breezed out, leaving a trio of shocked spectators.

Zack raised his eyebrows, completely befuddled. "What did I say?"

Charlie and Yvonne burst into laughter. "Maybe I should've introduced your project manager."

"What do you mean?"

Charlie pointed toward of the front door. "Liza Henderson is in charge of Blackwater Lake, your real-estate venture."

Zack groaned. "Oops. Kevin told me to talk to Henderson, but I assumed Henderson was a man. I guess that'll teach me to jump to conclusions."

"Liza's always had a way with words. She lost me with *unctuous,* but the jerk part I got." Charlie glanced at Yvonne.

She answered with a shrug.

"Not to get into understatement, but you guys seem to have gotten off on the wrong foot. How about we call a taxi to take you to your hotel? You can get cleaned up and have something to eat. Then if you're in the mood, I'll pick you up around six and take you out for the best catfish and hush puppies in the South. I'll explain everything then."

Zack rolled his head to relieve the crick in his neck. "A shower sounds like heaven. All I had for breakfast was a Twinkie, so I'm game."

After Zack left for the hotel, Yvonne strolled back into Charlie's office. "All right, what happened?"

"It looks like our ice princess cracked. When we were young, she was a little firecracker, but she mellowed after the girls were

born. And then after Rob disappeared she shut down emotionally."
Three years before, Rob Henderson had left to run an errand and
vanished. "I've never seen anyone get her riled up like that, not
even Rob and the kids. And they could test Gandhi's patience."

"When she yelled at you, I just about lost it."

"About time, don't you think? She's been building that pro-
tective wall for years. I was beginning to assume there wasn't any
way to break it. Whew." He swiped at his brow. "Remind me not
to make her mad." He flashed Yvonne a goofy grin. "Those two
appear to be like oil and water. *This* could be really interesting."

"Should I also remind you that Liza said she doesn't want
anything to do with him, or are you planning to persuade her
otherwise?"

Charlie's smirk was rife with false confidence. "I'm sure I can
talk her into it. If my considerable charm doesn't work, I'll try guilt.
Seriously, I have to make sure she's on board. I got a threatening
letter from those crazy murderers. The sheriff thinks I might be the
next target." His lightheartedness faded at the mention of the
crimes. "He suggested it might be wise for me to take a vacation."

"They really think you're at risk?" Yvonne asked.

"Yeah. The cops don't have anything concrete to go on, but
that's their latest assessment."

"Damn, I can't believe Bill Payton and Chris Carter are really
dead. What in the world's happening to our sleepy little town?"

"I wish I knew." Charlie grimaced. Not only were they his
friends, they'd been colleagues for years. "I'm going to miss
them." The two men had disappeared almost a month apart, and
their bodies had never been found. The perpetrators had sent
pictures of the remains to the media and notes threatening more
mayhem if development didn't stop. The police assumed there was
more than one murderer, simply because of the logistics of the
crimes. Bill Payton was a former football player. It would have
taken at least two people to subdue him. However, without a crime
scene or actual corpse, they were at a distinct disadvantage.

For years, Magnolia County, with its deep-water lake, had been popular with people from Atlanta who wanted a weekend retreat. As the city grew, and a long commute was the norm rather than the exception, development in Magnolia County had exploded. Apparently some folks had taken deadly umbrage at that turn of events.

Charlie parked himself in his leather chair. "It appears the crime spree is tied to something that happened years ago. I've racked my brain trying to figure out a common denominator, but the only thing that comes to mind is a public housing venture we all worked on in Atlanta." He made a tsking sound. "But that was fifteen years ago. The whole thing has me baffled."

"Too bad the police are as mystified as everyone else." Yvonne paused. "Do you suppose Liza could be in danger?"

"I don't think so. Sheriff Dave and I discussed it. We agreed that since she hasn't been in the business very long, the chances of the bad guys going after her are slim. Rob would be a different story. He was right in the middle of every project we managed."

Rob had been Charlie's original partner. And although Liza was a stay-at-home mom, she'd also worked part-time for Henderson and Taylor. So after Rob disappeared she'd naturally assumed his position in the business.

"Do you think Liza will ditch this project?" Yvonne asked.

"Are you kidding? Blackwater Lake is her baby. I'm not brave enough to talk her out of it, or to lay down the law." Although he meant his comment as a joke, Charlie was concerned about Liza. What if they were wrong about the murders being connected to something from the past?

"She is a mite stubborn, isn't she?"

"Yep, that she is." Charlie prayed Liza's tenacity wouldn't get her in trouble.

Chapter Five

Sleep, clean clothes and a shower had made a huge difference in Zack's attitude. He might live, after all.

"I'm glad you dressed casually," Charlie said when they met in the lobby of the Mimosa Inn. "I only wear a suit when I have a meeting with a lawyer."

Charlie kept up the chatter as they walked toward a Land Rover parked in the circular driveway. "Have you been to the sunny South before?"

"I've visited New Orleans, but that's about it."

Charlie drove out of the parking lot and headed down Main Street. "I'll give you the fifty-cent excursion, not that there's much to see in Magnolia Bluffs." Zack's windshield tour included the courthouse, the statue of Confederate General Joe Johnston, numerous antebellum homes and a flower-bedecked gazebo.

"Liza's twin sister owns that place." Charlie indicated a shop that was so girlie it made Zack's teeth ache.

"Miss Scarlett's Boudoir?"

"Yep. Maizie's cornered the market on froufrou. The women in town love it. Maizie's apparently a whiz at doing make-overs."

"Is that right." Just the mention of Liza Henderson piqued Zack's interest. "Is Liza's twin fraternal or identical?"

"Definitely fraternal. They're as different as night and day, in both looks and personality. Maizie is a Marilyn Monroe type—blond and voluptuous. And you've met Liza."

Yes, he had. She was the first woman in a long time to spark his libido, but for all he knew, she was married, and that meant she was off-limits. Angela had left him feeling like roadkill, so he wasn't ready to jump into anything new, anyway.

"The trees around here are really big," Zack said, attempting to change the subject.

"Yeah, some of our oaks are a couple of hundred years old," Charlie said. "Southerners are like the Chinese. We eat rice and worship our ancestors. Around here if you can't qualify for the Sons or Daughters of the Confederacy, you're SOL."

As the son of a welder-turned-real-estate tycoon and a high school English teacher, Zack supposed *he'd* be SOL.

"I'm taking you to a place that has cold beer and the best catfish in town. I have to warn you, though, it ain't pretty." Charlie pulled into the rutted parking lot of a building that appeared to be on its last legs.

"I take it the good old boys like it here." The lot was full of pickups with rifle racks.

"Yeah, and some yuppies, too." Charlie indicated a brand-new Lexus. "The food is just like my mom makes. But she's a church-going woman, and she won't let me drink at her house. So I come here instead."

The clatter of dishes battled with loud conversations and music from the jukebox. The smell of fried fish mingled with the spicy aroma of gumbo and jambalaya.

Charlie and Zack walked toward the back of the restaurant and found a booth in a relatively quiet corner. The green vinyl seats were cracked, and the music on the jukebox hailed from the time of the Four Tops. It reminded Zack of some of the joints he'd patronized in his youth.

His host's choice of dining establishment was interesting, to say the least. And if Zack's cop intuition wasn't on the fritz,

Charlie was gearing up for a serious discussion. He could tell something bad was going down, and it was undoubtedly more critical than the shooting and vandalism at the construction site.

After they ordered dinner, Charlie made small talk until he finally got to the heart of the matter. "I have to leave town for an indefinite period of time," he said. "But don't worry. Liza's incredible. You guys won't miss me."

Before Zack could say anything, Charlie explained the entire situation.

"That's it in a nutshell," he said when he'd finished. "I'm going to hide out at a friend's house for a couple of days, and then I'm on my way. When the cops tell you to get out of town, you listen."

"You're right." San Francisco law enforcement rarely got that involved. "Will we be able to reach you?"

"Sure." Charlie wrote his cell number on a napkin. "Call me anytime. But I'll probably be the one pestering you. Hiding out's bound to get old fast." He took another swig of beer. "I know your boss is concerned about everything that's happening out at the site. Honestly, I don't think you need to worry. And I truly don't believe it's related to this murder thing. If I did, I'd be getting us out of the Blackwater deal."

"Someone getting shot doesn't sound minor to me," Zack said, wondering how much to tell Charlie about his status in the company, but deciding to fill him in on the whole story. "In my real life, I'm a cop. Right now I'm on sabbatical." He smiled wryly. "I had a bit of a *Dirty Harry* episode, so my captain *suggested* I take a vacation until everything cooled off."

"*Dirty Harry,* as in Clint Eastwood's *Dirty Harry?*"

"Yep, I shot a suspect. It wasn't something I wanted to do, but it was a life-or-death situation," Zack said, not intending to provide any more information. "At any rate, Norton Development is a family business. So even though I don't actually work there, I have a financial interest. We decided that since I was at loose ends, I'd come check things out. I'd like to keep the fact I'm a policeman a secret for the moment. I'll stay in the background and get the lay of the land."

"I have to tell Liza. Is that a problem?"

"No, that's fine. But back to the problem at hand, the shooting."

Much to Zach's surprise, Charlie burst out laughing. "Let me explain. About six months back, we hired Linus Boatwell as a night watchman. He's not the brightest guy in town, but he's honest. I suspect he wandered off the beaten trail for a smoke break, and accidentally happened upon a poacher or someone with a still. They peppered his butt with buckshot."

"So, you don't think it was specifically directed at our development?"

"Not really."

Zack couldn't decide whether to believe that or not, but time would tell.

What he did know was that ever since his fracas with Liza Henderson, his curiosity had been running at top speed. "Do you think Mrs. Henderson will consent to work with me? She didn't sound too ambiguous last time I saw her."

"Don't worry. She's like putty in my hands," Charlie said, digging into the meal the waitress had just delivered.

"If I believed that, I'd buy some swampland from you."

"You already have. Bought swampland, that is," Charlie replied with a grin. "But don't worry. I'll make sure things with Liza are A-okay."

Zack nodded. "Why don't you call her now? I want to watch you work a miracle."

"I'll do that after dinner." Charlie obviously believed in delaying the inevitable.

"Okay, we can compromise. You call later, but right now I want you to give me the straight skinny on Mrs. Henderson."

With this beautiful grandmother, he needed *all* the help he could get.

Charlie wiped his face with a napkin.

"I don't feel comfortable discussing Liza's private life. What I can tell you is that her husband, Rob, and I started the firm. About three years ago, he disappeared. That's when Liza joined the partnership full-time."

"Disappeared?"

"Without a trace."

That meant she was unattached. Interesting! But was she qualified to handle such a large project?

"Regardless, let me assure you, she's a wonderful land-use attorney. And she's related to half the folks in town. In a place like Magnolia Bluffs, that's always a benefit. We're all really excited about this project, including Liza."

That was good to know, especially considering he and Kevin had a boatload of money at stake.

"She wasn't happy about old Linus picking buckshot out of his butt," Charlie said between bites.

"Neither are we—that's why I'm here. If we have a problem, we want to nip it in the bud," Zack said.

"Amen to that. I'm actually glad you're here. I'm fairly sure Liza will be okay, but having you around makes me feel better. You will keep her safe, won't you?"

"Absolutely." But as fiery and spunky as Mrs. Henderson appeared to be, she could probably take care of herself.

Chapter Six

Liza was at the back door of Maizie's boutique almost before the sun came up. It had been a long, sleepless night, and she desperately needed a heaping dollop of sisterly advice, accompanied by a cappuccino.

The gold-leaf sign on the window read Miss Scarlett's Boudoir, and if the inventory was any indication, Miss Scarlett had had herself a high old time. The residents of a New Orleans fancy house would have felt right at home surrounded by the lace pillows, frothy undergarments and frilly feminine apparel. Even the bell above the door sounded girlie. It was kitschy, it was funky and it was one of Liza's favorite places.

"For you to be here at seven o'clock, this has to be good," Maizie said as she got out of her lipstick-pink 1957 Mustang convertible. "Should I call Kenni to join us?" She held up her cell phone.

Kenni McAllister was their cousin. She was also a charter member of their indomitable trio.

Liza shook her head, eliciting a raised eyebrow from her twin. As much as she loved Kenni, this situation was embarrassing enough without having more people involved. Plus, her cousin was a newlywed. She had better things to do with her time.

"You'll never believe what I did yesterday!" Liza flopped on the red satin fainting couch, putting her head in her hands. "I am so embarrassed."

"Here." Maizie brought her a cup of coffee and sat down on the other end of the sofa. "Did you get a parking ticket?" she asked with a giggle.

Liza had a reputation for being the organized, reliable twin. And usually that was a fair assessment. Maizie, on the other hand, was known for her spontaneity.

"Did you run over the mayor, get booked on DUI charges or wear patent-leather shoes before Easter?"

"Maizie, get serious. I made such a fool of myself." Liza reached for the box of chocolate truffles Maizie kept on the coffee table. "With all the shenanigans going on out at the site, I've been afraid of what the California folks would do. Well, they sent a guy named Zack Maynard to check on us," she said, making her disdain clear. "So, yesterday I picked him up at the bus station."

"The bus station?"

"Uh-huh. I was PMSing and irritable as all get-out." She waved a hand in the air. "But that's no excuse for calling him an unctuous jerk."

"You did *what?*" Maizie asked.

"I called him an unctuous jerk. I think I also added *supercilious* and *punctilious* to my litany." Liza grimaced, remembering her tirade. "I went for a hat trick."

Her sister hooted with laughter and then leaned back with her coffee. "This I've got to hear. Spill it."

Liza started at the beginning. "Charlie asked me to pick the guy up. So while I was standing out front of the Magnolia Inn, looking like an Appalachian taxi driver and holding a stupid sign with his name on it, some redneck hit my truck."

"Oh, please tell me you weren't driving your rust bucket."

"I was. And I like my pickup."

"That's priceless. Keep going. This is getting good."

Liza's frown made Maizie laugh all the harder. "The hit-and-run driver knocked off my bumper."

Tears were running down Maizie's face.

"It's not funny."

"Oh, yes, it is," Maizie said, wiping her eyes.

"Then Mr. Maynard and I got in a fight over who would carry his suitcase and Booty Carter almost arrested us. But—" Liza paused "—the worst of it was that I waited until we had Charlie for an audience before I went bonkers." She moaned. "Oh, gawd! I don't know what got into me."

"This is wonderful. Simply marvelous."

"Yeah, right. I insulted the man who *owns* this project. The money guy! And I screamed at Charlie in front of God and everyone." Liza sniffed. "I've worked so hard to be calm and peaceful and sedate. Then I blew it right out of the water."

"Oh, sweetie." Maizie put her arms around her twin. "Sometimes you've got to say what you're thinking. And," she added with a grin, "I want to meet this guy. He sounds like just what you need."

Liza could see where this was going. Her entire family had been hounding her to start dating. And to that, her answer was no thanks. One broken heart was more than enough for a lifetime.

"What do you mean by that?"

Maizie shrugged one shoulder. "Nothing. What does he look like?"

Liza smacked her sister with a pillow. "It doesn't matter what he looks like." And if Maizie bought that, she'd believe in fairies. "The problem is that I have to apologize to Charlie. And you know how obnoxious he can be when he's right." The sisters had a history with Charlie, dating back to elementary school pranks and practical jokes.

"He won't let you off easy. That's for sure."

"I don't know what came over me. All of a sudden it seemed as if a shrew took over my body. I still can't believe some of the things that came out of my mouth."

"Here." Maizie handed her the cordless phone. "Call Charlie. I have to hear this."

Liza wanted to stick out her tongue, but she managed to control herself.

"Okay, okay." She took a deep breath, crossed her fingers and dialed the number before she could chicken out. Please God— let her get his voice mail.

"Charlie Taylor," the masculine voice barked.

Liza hesitated. "Hey, Charlie, this is your best friend."

"Really? I thought I'd been kicked out of that club. When did I get back in?"

"Listen, I, well, I was, uh, a little out of sorts yesterday. I think, um, I think I owe you and Mr. Maynard an apology."

"Have you reconsidered working with him?"

"Yes, I suppose so." Liza sighed. "There's something about him that bugs me. But I've worked with irritating people before, so I can do it again." She hoped her nose wasn't growing at the lie.

"I'll call him and set up a meeting for this afternoon. How does four-thirty at the bait shop work for you?"

"That's okay, but why are we meeting there instead of the office? That place is a dump."

"*That's* why. I'm keeping a low profile."

"Does this have to do with the murders?"

"Yeah. I'll tell you about it later. Are you coming to the office today?"

"I hadn't planned to. Do you need me?"

"No, but why don't you meet me an hour early. We should talk."

"Okay," she agreed, not liking the sound of that.

"I have another call. I'll see you this afternoon."

He disconnected before she could respond.

"That wasn't so bad, was it?" Maizie asked.

Liza wasn't quite sure. After that conversation, she was really worried about Charlie.

THE OLD BAIT SHOP WAS STUCK in a time warp. It still had the peeling paint and rusted sign that Liza remembered from her childhood. She hadn't been down to this part of the river since her daughters were little and Rob took them fishing on Sundays.

The interior hadn't changed much, either. The same neon beer signs, the same wooden booths, the same clientele and the same fragrant smell of frying onions and the pungent tang of fresh fish. When Liza's eyes adjusted to the dim interior, she spotted Charlie hunkered down in a booth at the rear of the café.

He was one of her oldest friends. Not only had they gone through school together, Charlie had introduced her to Rob their first year of college. She remembered it as if it were yesterday. The two guys had been lurking outside their freshman English class, checking out girls, when Liza had sort of accidentally mowed Rob down.

Knocking him on his butt wasn't exactly subtle, but it worked. That day she got the attention of the best-looking guy she'd ever laid eyes on. Within a year, they were married. They'd been so in love. In fact, they'd been in love right up to the end. That was why Liza refused to believe he'd left them voluntarily. He simply wouldn't have done it. In her heart, she knew he was dead, but the law said differently.

Charlie looked up from his beer. "Hey, kiddo. How's my best girl?"

Liza leaned over to kiss his cheek before taking a seat on the opposite bench. "Should I apologize now, or can I just wait and do it all at once when Mr. Maynard gets here? Eating crow is not my idea of a good time."

"You don't have to apologize to me. I thought it was funny. Besides, you're cute when you get all riled up."

"I feel so stupid." Liza felt herself blush at the admission. "I haven't lost my cool like that since I smacked Butter Bean McGruder in the eighth grade."

"That *was* a classic. I have to tell you, I think you should lose your temper more often." As Charlie took another sip of beer, his demeanor turned from jovial to serious. "There's something I have to tell you," he said, putting his elbows on the table.

"That sounds ominous."

"It is." Charlie told her what he knew about the murders. He also filled her in on Sheriff Dave's assumption that he might be the next target.

"That's why we're meeting here. I have to stay out of sight. I'll be leaving town, probably tomorrow. But I'll have my cell with me all the time. We won't be out of touch." He took her hand. "Promise me you'll be careful. I'm going to be worried sick about you."

"I'll be fine. Honestly, I will. Where are you heading off to?" Liza rubbed her forehead. If she pressed really hard, maybe the monster headache would stop in its tracks.

"Europe, Australia, Asia—I don't know. All I know is that I don't plan to die. At least, not yet." He tried to break the dark mood with a wink.

"God, Charlie, I'm not sure what to say." She moved over to his side of the table. The man needed a hug. *She* needed a hug!

"Please be careful. If you think we need to get out of the Blackwater Lake project, you have my blessing. Money isn't everything," he said.

"I know. If things get dicey, I'll ditch it." That might be easier said than done. Quitting wasn't in her repertoire. "And don't worry about Mr. Maynard. I'll be so helpful he'll be ready to go back to San Francisco, just like that." She snapped her fingers.

"I hope you're right. Seriously, I think it'd help if you'd call him Zack. Believe it or not, he's really a nice guy."

"He sure's a handsome devil, I'll give him that much. The nice part is debatable."

"Is that right? You think I'm good-looking?"

There was no doubt about the owner of that rich baritone. Darn! Why couldn't the floor open up and swallow her? Somehow the handsome devil himself had managed to sneak in and was now standing next to the booth in all his handsomeness. When *would* she learn to control her mouth?

Charlie didn't miss a beat as he stood to shake Zack's hand. "Please sit down. I want to formally introduce you to my friend, my business partner and your project manager—Liza Henderson."

Chapter Seven

"Maizie, are you here?" It was the morning after the bait-shop debacle and Liza was back at the boutique for another dose of chocolate, cappuccino and sisterly commiseration. Liza would rather eat worms than admit she was discombobulated by a guy, but there it was.

"Hey, sugar, whatcha up to? And what's with the dress?" Maizie asked as she sashayed in from the back room. "Did someone die?" She clutched her chest in mock consternation.

Liza gave her a saccharine-sweet smile. "Cute. I'm, uh, going out to lunch.

"With?"

Although Liza was in dire need of sympathy, she was hesitant to tell Maizie about her latest foot-in-mouth episode.

"With Zack Maynard. I thought I should look professional. I need a little help from you."

"You came to the right place." Maizie led her over to the mirror and snapped a pink plastic cape in the air. She was wearing her smug know-it-all expression—the one Liza hated.

"Sit down, sweetie, I'm gonna give you some extra armor, not that you need it, now, ya hear, but it's always better to go into battle fully prepared." Maizie unzipped her cosmetics case and waved a mascara wand in the air. "This is my sword."

Maizie was known throughout the county for her makeovers.

She was also famous for the fact that she wore her Miss Peach Blossom tiara every chance she got. According to Mama, the girl would want to be buried in the darn thing. But Mama should talk—she'd be meeting Saint Peter in a pink Chanel suit with a matching pillbox hat. As far as Eleanor Westerfield was concerned, Jackie Kennedy was the last woman in the White House to have a lick of fashion sense.

"I'm not sure about this," Liza complained. In true sisterly fashion, Maizie ignored her and continued to slather on the goop.

"Hush up, now. Mama already thinks you're a changeling." She applied a coat of eyeliner.

"Let me look." Maizie checked out her handiwork. "Close, but I'm not quite finished." She dug through her case for an eye shadow that wouldn't clash with Liza's red tunic dress. "And I want details about this guy who has your knickers in a twist— other than that you went bonkers in front of him."

"There aren't any details. None. Zero. Zip. Nada. We've only met twice, and both times he's made me mad enough to spit nails," Liza claimed as she pawed through the lipstick samples.

"And is this zero, zip, nada guy good-looking?"

"Beyond belief. Damn!"

Maizie had the nerve to laugh.

"And you can stop looking like that. I'm not interested in any man. In forty years they'll be talking about the crazy old lady with all the animals. Besides, he's too young for me."

"How old is he?"

"I don't know. But he's definitely younger than I am."

Maizie laughed again. "Young, schmoung. If he's over thirty-five he's fair game. And who said anything about marrying him? Legally, you can't do anything—not for another year at least. And Mama would die if you got hitched to someone from *San Francisco!* We're talking sex. Hot, wild sex." She put her hands on her rounded hips. "Your problem is that you jump to conclusions without getting all the facts.

Remember the time you thought Ted Hopkins was having an affair with Amanda Short because his truck was parked in her driveway every day at noon? And all he was doing was tiling her rec room."

Liza was still focused on the thought of hot, wild sex.

Maizie pulled the cape off Liza's shoulders and ran a brush through her twin's glossy black bob. "I don't care if this is a business lunch, I'm horning in. I want to see him." She fluffed her own curly blond hair. "Maybe he's my type."

"Yeah, right."

Maizie had been married to the same guy for twenty years.

"By the way, have you made it over to Miss Landry's to get measured for your bridesmaid's dress?" Maizie asked in a lightning-fast non sequitur.

That was an errand Liza would rather forget. "Yes, I did. I still can't believe our cousin, or second cousin, or whatever she is, is having a big church wedding. It's her fourth, for goodness' sake. And furthermore, I can't believe we agreed to participate."

"Well, hon, you know how Vivian is. She was a diva when we were in kindergarten." Maizie's grin widened. "Did Miss Landry show you a picture of our dresses?"

That grin wasn't a good omen. "No." Liza paused, waiting for her sister to continue, but the twit simply giggled. Good God! "What? What does the fruitcake have up her sleeve now?"

"Hoopskirts. Pink satin hoopskirts."

"Nope. No, no, no! I won't do it."

"You've got to. It's too late to find anyone else who's short enough to walk down the aisle with Clarence Pierpoint. And Clarence is the groom's brother, so he has to be a groomsman. That means you're stuck."

Liza groaned. Somehow she'd managed to fall into a hoop-skirted hell. And while that was bad enough, it didn't hold a candle to her real problems—Zack Maynard and the situation at the Blackwater Lake project. She had the feeling something earth-shaking was about to happen. Unfortunately, she didn't have a clue whether it was her body or her heart that was in danger.

Chapter Eight

Zack couldn't seem to get Liza Henderson out of his mind and that was the last thing he needed. He had enough swirling around in his brain as it was, which brought him back to his current assignment—ferreting out what was happening at Blackwater Lake.

This would be his first meeting with Liza without Charlie there to act as a buffer. Their previous encounters had been interesting, if tempestuous. So how would this one play out?

Zack was happy to walk to Liza's office. A trip to the car-rental place was definitely in order, but this stroll gave him the perfect opportunity to think about his situation and to take stock of the town.

Magnolia Bluffs could pass for a movie set. Huge oaks dripping Spanish moss created a shady canopy over Main Street. It was a tranquil place where locals stopped to gossip on the sidewalk, and dogs lounged outside their owners' shops. The white lattice bandstand in the city park provoked images of hoop-skirted belles and Fourth of July picnics.

In this frothy world of honeysuckle and azaleas, antique stores and boutiques vied with restaurants and professional offices in the downtown area.

Zack stopped on the brick sidewalk and took a visual survey of the cottage housing the offices of Taylor and Henderson. This morning, instead of a cat lounging on the wicker settee, there was a huge yellow dog taking a nap, his head resting on his paws.

He squatted to ruffle the pup's ears. "You like that, don't you?" The canine's tail vigorously thumped up and down.

Liza had apparently heard Zack's voice through the open window, and she joined him on the porch, sitting on the top step. "His name is P.B., short for Peanut Butter. He's a golden retriever, so needless to say, he's not much of a watchdog. The dope would probably show the burglar the family silver, but he's my special buddy, aren't you, boy?"

The dog rested his head in her lap.

"When he gets in the car I can't get him out, so he comes to work with me. I have quite a menagerie at home. In addition to this guy—" she gave P.B. another ear rub "—I also have a poodle named Jelly Belly and two horses. The ponies belong to my grandsons. They're my buddies."

P.B. responded with another tail thump.

Zack sat down with her. "Does he grin all the time?"

"He's a happy dog," Liza said, standing to brush off her dress.

"What happened to the cat?" Zack asked.

"What cat?"

"The one that was sleeping on the porch the other day."

For a second, Liza looked confused. "Oh, you mean Clover. She lives next door and sometimes she strolls over for a visit."

"Oh."

"Let's go in. I'll introduce you to the rest of the staff." She winced, but recovered quickly, leading him into the cottage.

Zack didn't miss her slight tremor, and he knew she was thinking about her showstopping meltdown the last time he'd been here. He also didn't overlook the fact that she was gorgeous. *Stop it!* No ogling allowed. Yeah, right, Zack thought as he followed her into the foyer.

On his previous visit he'd been so wiped out not much had registered. This time he really took stock of his surroundings. At first glance the reception area looked like a comfortable living room with shiny hardwood floors and ornately carved molding.

Burgundy leather sofas flanked a fireplace, creating a welcoming spot for a meetings or an intimate chat.

Fresh flowers in a crystal vase sat on the table against the far wall. Opposite the fireplace was a large cherry table and matching chairs. It was a cozy and comfortable work environment.

"You've met Yvonne." Liza indicated the blond receptionist he'd met the day before.

"I certainly did. How are you doing?"

"Just fine, thank you." She wiggled her fingers in what Zack realized was the Southern way of saying hello.

"Would you like a tour of our facilities before we meet Ruben Jones? He's going to be working part-time on the project."

"Sure," Zack agreed, following Liza down the central hall to the kitchen, the obvious heart of the business. Filing cabinets, a copy machine, a fax machine and a wall of law books and blueprints lined the room. A large skylight caught every possible ray of sun. This was a world away from Zack's grimy cubicle at the precinct.

"I thought we'd go to the bakery for lunch. Ruben's out on a job site, but he said he'd meet us there. Is that okay with you?"

Zack was so hungry he'd eat wallpaper paste. Plus, he'd already figured out that Southerners usually did business over some sort of meal. "That's fine, but if we have to drive, I'm out of luck. I still need to find a car-rental place."

"Everything's within walking distance, except the shopping center out on the highway. But after lunch, I'll take you to rent a car."

The neighborhood they strolled through was a hodgepodge of palatial antebellum homes and smaller bungalows. Live oaks, magnolias, camellias and azaleas were the only visible common denominator.

They'd walked several blocks down Main Street before Liza stopped in front of an old-fashioned storefront. "Here's the bakery," she said, opening the door.

The sweet smell of cinnamon and the rich aroma of roasted

coffee drifted out. They were both wonderful reminders of Zack's mom's kitchen. His parents had divorced when he was only three. His mother had reverted to her maiden name and moved back to the family farm in Kansas. His dad had gone to California and made a fortune in construction.

In many ways, Magnolia Bluffs wasn't all that different from where Zack had grown up in Kansas. He hadn't moved to San Francisco until he went to college.

After ordering lunch, Zach chose a table and sat down to watch the activity on the sidewalk. Liza was busy chatting with the girl at the counter. A woman pushing a stroller with a black Lab in tow stopped in front of the window to talk to a silver-haired matron. This was déjà vu of home. There was a distinct absence of hustle and bustle. Only the teenagers seemed to be in a hurry, and God alone knew where they were going.

It would take a while for him to slip into the slow and easy pace of life in Georgia. He wasn't even sure Magnolia Bluffs and San Francisco existed in the same universe.

Zack's attention turned to a voluptuous—so sue him, he was a guy—blonde stepping out of a bright pink 1957 Mustang. He couldn't decide which he found more attractive—the car or the woman. It was that guy thing again.

LIZA NOTICED MAIZIE getting out of that ridiculous car of hers and plastered a phony smile on her face. It was time to dredge up her best Cotillion manners. She had specifically warned her sister to leave them alone for lunch—not that Maizie ever listened.

"Hey, sweetie, imagine meeting you here," Maizie said, loud enough for half the patrons in the bakery to hear.

"Yeah, really," Liza responded in a normal tone of voice. "One of these days, I'm gonna get you," she whispered as she pulled Maizie toward the table where Zack was sitting.

"Mr. Maynard, this is my sister, Maizie Walker. That's short for Mary Stuart. My real name is Elizabeth. Our mother had a thing about English royalty. I suppose I'm lucky she didn't name me George." Liza realized she was babbling, but she couldn't control herself.

"We're twins, even though we don't look anything alike, but you can see that, can't you?" Liza waved a hand in Maizie's direction. Damn—more blather. "Anyway, she was born first, but only by a few minutes. She claims that makes her older and wiser." What was *wrong* with her? She sounded like Sister Truegood at the Evangelical Church when she was speaking in tongues.

Zack had stood when they'd walked up. One side of his mouth was twitching as if he was trying to conceal his amusement. Swear to goodness, if the man laughed, Liza would have to smack him.

"Glad to meet you, Miss Maizie," he said, displaying a sexy, dimpled smile that he'd never bothered to aim at Liza.

Then it hit her: he *really* didn't like her. Who could blame him? While Liza was fantasizing about hot sex, the primary player in her erotic fantasy couldn't get past her lapse of decorum. Okay, she'd blown it. So, on to plan B—the one where she presented herself as the ultimate professional.

Liza was going to be spending a ton of time with the guy, so she'd have to overlook everything he said or did—or didn't do. A competent Southern belle could brazen her way through just about any situation—even dealing with Mr. Sexy on a daily basis. *This* was going to be a true test of her Steel Magnolia capabilities.

"Maizie, is it hot in here to you?" Liza picked up a menu and fanned her face.

Her sister smirked. "Nope. In fact, I'm a bit chilly."

Liza wanted to flip her off, but a lady would never do that. If Maizie didn't stop her irritating simpering, Liza was afraid she'd lose it. And if the woman fluttered her eyelashes one more time— twin or no twin—she was gonna regret it. Giggle, flutter, cleavage adjustment—that did it.

"Did you know my sister's been happily married for twenty years?"

Zack smiled at Maizie. "That's great. You must've been a child bride."

"Not really. We married after we both graduated from the University of Georgia. I was a teacher. I have a daughter at UGA now."

"You look much too young for all that."

Liza resisted the urge to scream.

Chapter Nine

Zack watched the emotions flicker across Liza's expressive face. She'd make a lousy poker player. There was something about her that got his juices flowing. Too bad he'd sworn off women, at least until he had the Angela situation under control.

"Liza, sugar, I've got to head off to the shop. Zack, it was a real pleasure meeting you." Maizie hugged them both before sashaying out the door.

"Does she flirt with everyone?" Zack realized he'd asked a very un–PC question, but for some reason he was dying to hear Liza's answer.

"Flirting's in her blood. It's like breathing."

"What about you?"

"I'm the practical one in the family."

What was she like when she was off the clock? He'd had a glimpse of that woman, and he'd liked it—too much.

"Here's Ruben," she said, short-circuiting his more libidinous thoughts.

The man making his way through the tables put Zack in mind of Ichabod Crane—tall, gaunt and ascetic.

Liza introduced them, and after the requisite niceties, they got down to business.

"I understand you're here because of the trouble we've been having," Ruben said.

"Yes, primarily." Zack deliberately kept his response vague.

"Can you tell us exactly what your boss thinks you'll be able to do?" Liza asked.

Thinking about Kevin's expectations—not that Kevin was his boss—Zack answered quickly. "He wants to figure out whether the troubles are a glitch or a symptom of something bigger."

Liza looked as if she was deciding how much to tell him. He hoped she wouldn't try to B.S. him.

"Okay, here's all we know. We've been dealing with folks from a small congregation called the Spirit of the Holy Protector. Rumor has it they practice a strange mixture of Santeria and Fundamentalism. My uncle Dave, the sheriff, thinks they're snake handlers. He also suspects they grow pot to use in their services, but he's never been able to prove it. My theory is that the vandalism happened because our surveying crew got too close to their marijuana fields and they decided to do take action."

"Snake handlers, marijuana fields?" The folks in this town were beyond nutty. "So why do they object to Blackwater Lake?"

Liza's expression said, "Duh!" but she politely refrained from uttering the word. "Blackwater Lake is adjacent to their property and they're not happy about having more than a thousand new neighbors. When Georgia Pacific owned the land, they had trouble with people messing with the equipment. So it doesn't seem like a stretch to assume the same individuals would try mischief with us."

"That would explain the problems the consultants encountered." After months spent mapping the site all traces of the technicians' work had mysteriously been destroyed. Thousands and thousands of dollars were wasted, not to mention the time involved repeating the process. And in the real-estate business, time was money.

"As for the shooting," Liza continued, "I think Linus got too close to the pot fields. But I honestly don't know what the church people are capable of doing. Maybe we need to do a stakeout and see if we can catch someone."

Was she serious? Amateurs! They all thought they were qualified to deal with criminal investigations. Little Miss Nancy Drew needed to be disabused of that notion, but chastising her wasn't the way to do it. On to a safer topic.

"Tell me about the permit process and the politics involved." Before Zack had left San Francisco, Kevin had given him a crash course in Real Estate 101. He hoped he knew enough to not sound like a total idiot.

"We're stalled," Liza admitted, running her fingers through her hair. "For the project to go ahead, the Board of Supervisors has to vote to change the zoning. Right now it's designated as agricultural. Obviously, we need to get them on our side." This time, her grin seemed sincere. "Are you ready to schmooze your way to success?"

Zack could be charming when he had to be. "Sure. I just need a tutorial on the local situation."

Ruben jumped into the conversation. "Here's the deal. The Board of Supervisors has three members, so obviously we need the support of two of them. We have a former schoolteacher, a guy Liza claims is a pervert and a Birkenstock-wearing earth mother."

"Sounds like quite a combo."

Ruben laughed. "Liza's favorite is G. Harry Middleton."

"The man's a sicko." Liza made a face. "The women who work in his office suspect he spends his days looking up porn sites on the Internet."

"Although Liza doesn't like good old G. Harry, we still have to court him."

"Not me. He makes my skin crawl." Liza emphasized her statement with a gagging sound.

Ruben gave her a sly grin. "We'd better keep Liza away from G. Harry. I'm afraid she might try to make mountain oysters out of his privates."

Zack suppressed a flinch. "You guys are going to have to walk me through this minefield. When do we start and what's the next step?"

"I'll call a meeting with our subcontractors," Liza said. "We'll do a site visit tomorrow. The surveyors have almost finished—for the second time. By the way, did you bring hiking boots and jeans?"

"Uh-huh." He couldn't wait to ditch the suit and tie.

"Are you planning to stay at the Mimosa Inn?" Ruben asked.

"That's my plan."

"What do you think about seeing whether Auntie Em has a cottage available?" Liza directed her question to Ruben, and then returned her attention to Zack. "It's close to the office and very private."

"I don't know." Ruben cleared his throat. "Em's place is, uh, awfully pink. And she can be a mite overwhelming."

Zack kept silent. The exchange between Liza and Ruben didn't allow room for anyone else's opinion. This Southern thing—the struggle to outdo each other in the kindness department—was both entertaining and infectious.

"Don't listen to him," Liza told Zack, throwing a chiding look at Ruben. "Emily Harrison has a bed-and-breakfast with three lovely guest cottages. Everyone in town calls her Auntie Em." She shot him a grin. "It's a bit over-the-top, but it's close to everything, and Auntie Em's a great cook."

"A bit over-the-top," Ruben retorted. "It's so pink and frilly, it takes my breath away, but Liza's right. It's not far from our office, and she'll treat you like a long-lost grandson."

Zack wasn't sure he was cut out to live in a Victoria's Secret closet, but he was flexible. "That'll be fine. How do I make a reservation?"

"I'll call her. I'm sure there won't be a problem," Ruben said. "After we eat, I'll take you to a car-rental place. I'll bet you'll be glad to have your own transportation, won't you?"

She didn't know the half of it. In order to do any kind of effective investigation, Zack not only needed a car but he was going to have to restock his arsenal of equipment. Including a weapon.

Chapter Ten

Early the next morning Zack headed back to Liza's office. He'd spent a restless night worrying about the upcoming meeting with the subcontractors. He finally decided his best option was to go with the "when in doubt keep you mouth shut" theory. Hopefully, that'd do the trick. Getting up to speed was not going to be an easy task.

P.B. was sitting on the front porch, thumping his tail. "Enjoying life, huh?" he asked the pooch. Much to his surprise, someone responded.

"If you rub his tummy, he'll be your friend forever."

Zack hadn't noticed Liza sitting on the wicker settee with a glass of iced tea in her hand. "I can do that." He squatted to vigorously scratch P.B.'s stomach.

"Come on in. We'll get you something cold to drink. It's only spring, but it's already getting hot."

Zack trailed her to the kitchen.

"If you have your stuff with you, I'll take you over to the B and B," she said, pouring iced tea into a frosty tumbler. "Then you can get settled before our afternoon meeting."

"Sounds like a plan."

WHEN ZACK SAW the B and B, he thought *frilly* was a serious understatement. It looked more like a set for Alice in Wonderland's tea party. All the elements were there—a Victorian house with gleaming white shutters, a picket fence, azaleas in various hues of pink, an orange tabby sunning on the wraparound porch and an angelic white-haired woman who belonged in a Norman Rockwell painting.

"Quaint, isn't it?" Liza asked when she joined him at the gate.

"Yeah, well."

"Are you chicken?" she teased. "Let's go meet Auntie Em." She grabbed his hand, pulling him up the steps.

"Looks like you could use some of my cooking, young man. Come in, come in." Auntie Em scooted the enormous cat out of the way with her foot. "Move, Horace. Let's go in and have some tea and goodies. Then Liza can take you out to see the cottage." Auntie Em led them into the parlor. "This is probably a little flowery for you," she said, tweaking his cheek. "It drove my late husband crazy. He wanted a room all done up in leather. The silly man liked the smell of cigar smoke."

The parlor was a botanical haven of pink, rose and red. Flower-printed fabric and wallpaper covered every surface. A delicate English tea set was displayed on a chintz ottoman. Built-in shelves housed a lifetime collection of china, books and porcelain. Zack hadn't seen anything like this since his favorite cousin had made him play dolls with her when they were six years old. He could almost feel his testosterone quaking in fear.

"I hope you're not allergic to cats. Heidi thinks my guests are fair game." A calico jumped into Zack's lap and curled up. He hadn't been around cats for years; Angela hadn't wanted animals in the house. She said they were unsanitary. She'd had the same attitude about kids. Too bad she hadn't bothered to share that sentiment until after they were married.

"I put you in the Rosebud Cottage. It's quite private. There's even a separate driveway." Auntie Em kept up a monologue as she poured the tea.

What were the chances of actually falling down Alice's rabbit hole? In this place, pretty damned good.

ROSEBUD COTTAGE was a mini-version of the Victorian. Zack hoped to goodness it didn't have the same decor. He wasn't sure he'd be able to sleep in a Pepto-Bismol-pink bedroom. He gave the porch swing a push. "I haven't seen one of these in a long time."

While he was fumbling in his pocket for the key, Liza turned the knob.

"I didn't think she'd lock the door. Magnolia Bluffs used to be safe."

"Don't kid yourself, lady, there's crime everywhere."

"Until recently, I would've disagreed," Liza admitted. "We thought we had a murder last year, but it turned out to be a tragic accident. These murders are out of my realm of understanding."

"They would be for most people, but there's evil everywhere. It just takes the right circumstance for it to come out." And Zack had seen more than his share during his tenure in the homicide division. This didn't seem like the proper venue for that discussion, however, so he followed her inside.

He stopped dead in his tracks. Somehow he'd landed in the middle of a life-size Barbie Dream House. Pink walls, white wicker furniture and pillows of every shape and shade of— what else—pink!

"Yeah, yeah, I know." Liza made a sweeping gesture to encompass the interior. "This isn't very macho, but it has everything you'll need. And you'll get used to the color scheme."

Liza stifled a giggle as he glared at the pile of frilly throw pillows. She peered into several of the cupboards, obviously hoping to distract him with inane chatter. "She even stocked the refrigerator."

"Are you always this snoopy, or is this a special occasion?" Zack asked as Liza wandered into the bedroom.

She ignored him and continued her inspection. The bed looked like a fluffy white cloud covered with lace pillows.

"Oh, wow, this is fantastic. The mosquito netting may be a bit much, but otherwise it's great." Somehow she managed not to break into gales of laughter. That couldn't have been an easy feat considering the clear revulsion on Zack's face. He suspected this was the most fun she'd had in ages.

Liza had meandered into the bathroom and was rhapsodizing about the huge claw-foot tub, but Zack couldn't take his eyes off the bed. It immediately brought to mind sultry Southern nights, rumpled sheets and Liza, her silky black hair spread out across the pillow. He'd better get a grip. If she had any inkling, she'd either box his ears or run screaming to the car. She sure as heck wouldn't be taking him into the woods.

"Oh, look at this, you even have a bidet." To his relief she kept up a travelogue worthy of *Architectural Digest*.

In his current frame of mind he wasn't particularly interested in bidets, or the benefits of matching towels and sheets. In fact it was past time to get out of the bedroom.

"This will be fine. I'll get settled, and I'll be back at your office by two." The minute she left, he checked out the cold water in the shower.

Chapter Eleven

Before heading back to Liza's office, Zack spent an hour on the phone with Kevin. Millions of dollars were at stake and it was his job to make sure everything was A-okay. Zack intended to give it his best shot, at least until the politicos in the San Francisco Police Department got their heads out of their collective butts and let him get back to his real job.

He'd lost track of time so he was late for the meeting. A group of men were already sitting in the conference room, a pile of maps and drawings littering the table and floor.

Liza was seated at the head of the table. "Guys, this is Zack Maynard. He's from the San Francisco office." She introduced him to the assembled geo-techs, water specialists and planners. Each of the consultants then explained the county's requirements and the work they'd already finished. Zack was thinking about the expense involved while Liza provided a quick synopsis of everything that still needed to be done.

"If there isn't anything else, we'll go on out to the site," she said, addressing the entire group. Then she turned to Zack. "Most of these guys drove up from Atlanta, so we need to take a separate car. Do you want to drive, or do you want me to?"

Zack's last experience with her rust-mobile hadn't been all that enjoyable. "I'll drive."

"YOU MIGHT WANT TO SLOW DOWN. The lane's not much bigger than a path so it's hard to find." Liza scouted the woods for the turnoff. "Take a left just after the bend in the road, I think. Darn, I should've let the engineers lead. They know this area better than I do. They've certainly spent a lot of time out here."

As they bumped down the rutted lane, blackberry vines scraped the side of Zack's rented Expedition.

"That's why I have a beater truck," Liza said with a chuckle. "Pull over in the clearing ahead. We'll have to walk from here. There's a path down to the lake."

Zack had seen aerial and on-site photos of the property, but neither did justice to the lush beauty he encountered. Clusters of live oak and magnolia intermingled with the forest of pine trees that provided a habitat for a hundreds of migratory birds that visited every year.

"This is terrific." Zack was honestly impressed.

They spent over an hour hiking the land that would eventually be a village, a nature preserve and the first and second phases of housing. The consultants talked him through the blueprints and the maps of their work, but it was still all Greek to him.

He'd nearly maxed out on technical information when the lead engineer, Paul, brought up yet another problem. "The lakeshore is eroding. We'll eventually have to put in a retaining wall. If you two are up to it, Pete and I'd like to show you the area. It's not an easy hike, but it's not too far from here."

He addressed the technicians. "You guys can go back to town."

Zack extended a hand to help Liza up from the log she was sitting on. The second their fingers touched, a strange current surged through him.

She immediately dropped his hand. Interesting! He was almost positive she'd rather have a lobotomy than admit she'd felt the same zing.

Paul was right when he'd told them it would be rough going,

Zack thought a few minutes after they headed out. But what he hadn't said was that it would be akin to a survival trek.

"Are you okay?" Zack asked Liza. She looked delicate, but he suspected she was as tough as she had to be.

"Yeah, I'm—" She broke off as a large piece of bark hit her on the cheek. Then Zack heard three pings in rapid succession. Crap! That was gunfire.

He grabbed Liza around the waist, sending them both sliding toward the water.

"Get down! Someone's shooting at us!" he yelled, trying to warn the engineers.

"Stay still. Maybe they can't see us over here," he muttered, covering Liza with his body.

"I see you like bein' on top." As soon as the words were out, Liza clamped her mouth shut, a furious blush staining her cheeks.

Zack forced himself to focus on the situation at hand. "Let's be really still for a few more seconds." There was silence, blessed silence. Even the bullfrogs were quiet.

"Hang on to my waist. I'm going to roll us over behind the log," he whispered. "That'll give us better protection."

THAT SOUNDED LIKE A PLAN to her. It wasn't exactly a bulletproof bunker, but at this point, Liza would take any port in a storm. She wrapped her arms around him and burrowed her face in his chest, ready for the ride.

When they stopped rolling, Liza heard someone whisper, "Hey, you guys. Are you okay?" It was Paul. Thank goodness he was alive.

"Yeah, where are you?" Zack answered.

"Two trees over. Pete's closer to the water."

Liza wished they had more protection than a log—something with bullets would be nice.

"Stay where you are. I'm calling 911. We'll see how fast the cops can get out here," Zack instructed, punching in the numbers on his cell.

Somehow, despite all their rolling around, he'd managed to stay on top of Liza. He smiled down at her while tucking an errant lock of hair behind her ear. "How are you doing?"

Considering they were probably being shot at by some half-baked, pot-growing religious fanatic, and she was lying fully clothed under a gorgeous 190-pound male, she supposed she was okay. At least she wasn't seeing double or spurting blood. "I'm fine," she muttered.

"Sure?"

"Sure." There were those darn dimples of his again. "Now do you think you could roll off? You're squashing me." So what if that wasn't quite true?

He gave her a lazy smile before he complied.

It was almost fifteen minutes before they heard a siren.

"They must've made a stop at the Krispy Kreme," Liza muttered. "And they probably sent Stumpy Carter. He's Booty Carter's brother. He isn't the brightest guy in town, if you know what I mean. But still, I'd hate for him to get killed. Did you tell the dispatcher that someone was taking potshots at us?"

"Yep."

Liza heard a car door slam, and thank goodness there wasn't a responding sound of gunfire. If luck was with them, their assailant would already be at the tavern sipping a brew.

"Where are you folks?" An overweight cop in a Smokey hat stood at the edge of the ravine peering over.

"We're down here, Stumpy. Are you sure it's safe to be standing there? You're a perfect target."

"Darn, Liza, ain't nobody gonna shoot old Stump. Y'all come on up and let me get a statement."

Liza glanced at Zack, who gave her an eloquent shrug. Apparently he thought that if old Stump wasn't going to get nailed, they wouldn't, either.

"Okay, we'll be up in a minute," Zack yelled, helping Liza to her feet.

AFTER THEY TALKED TO STUMPY and gave him a brief statement, Zack and Liza returned to his SUV. He put his foot on the running board to remove his boot and banged it against the tire to get rid of the worst of the dirt.

"I feel like I've been in a mud-wrestling contest."

"Me, too." Liza took off her shoes and beat them on the ground. She caught a glimpse of herself in the side mirror. "Oh my God! You didn't tell me I had a huge smear of mud across my forehead." She licked a finger and dabbed at her face.

"It adds character," Zack said, barely managing to hide his grin. To be totally truthful, she looked darned cute.

"Yeah, right." Liza brushed her rear several times before hoisting herself up into the cab of the SUV. "I hope I don't ruin your seats." She leaned back against the leather and sighed. "I can't believe everything that's been happening."

Zack couldn't, either. What was supposed to be a quick fact-finding trip to the hinterlands had somehow evolved into a far more dangerous venture. First thing in the morning he intended to locate a gun shop, and then the sheriff's office. But right now, he was starving.

"Is there someplace we can go for a good burger?" Zack flicked at the mud on his jeans.

"The DeLite Diner. They have the best greasy burgers in Georgia." Liza pulled a mirror out of her purse and was working on the smudge on her face. "It's a truckers' haven." She gestured at her mud-splattered jeans. "We'll fit right in."

Draped in neon and shiny aluminum siding, the DeLite Diner was perched like a prettied-up drag queen on the side of the highway. Pickups, four-by-fours, cop cars and eighteen-wheelers were abundant in the parking lot.

"It's a popular place," Zack commented.

"That's because it's meat loaf night. And since we're getting here before five o'clock, we're eligible for the blue plate special.

Believe it or not, this is nothing compared to the crowd when they feature fried chicken. I didn't realize it before, but I'm ravenous."

"It's the adrenaline. That'll do it every time."

The diner was a beehive of noise and activity. "I see a place in the far back." Liza led the way to a small table next to the kitchen, stopping along the way to speak to people.

She picked up a menu that was sitting between the sugar shaker and the jukebox. "The burgers are good. The chili is a five-star heartburn waiting to happen, but if you're into sprouts you're out of luck." She handed him the other menu. "It looks like we're in Mavis's section." Liza hid behind her menu. "She's a real bitch."

A middle-aged woman in a stained white apron barreled toward them carrying a coffeepot and two mugs. "Want coffee?" She placed the cups on the table.

Despite a number of job-related commendations for bravery, Zack was almost afraid to refuse. "Sure, why not."

"No coffee, thanks," Liza said with a smile. "I'll have an iced tea."

After the waitress had stalked off, Zack leaned forward and whispered, "She acted like you ordered hemlock."

"Wait till you see her scowl if we order anything other than the special," Liza murmured. "And get ready, because I'm having a hamburger."

"I don't know if I'm that daring," Zack admitted, watching the hulking waitress march from table to table. "I'll stick to the meat loaf."

ZACK POLISHED OFF his meal and had started on dessert by the time Liza wiped up a dollop of ketchup with her last French fry.

"Mavis is in love with you. You ordered the coconut cream pie. Leave her a big tip and she's all yours."

"The food was good. It reminds me of home." Zack took another bite of the huge piece of pie Mavis had put in front of him.

"Where'd you grow up?"

"Kansas."

"Really?" she asked. "I thought you were from California."

"I went to college in the Bay Area, but I'm originally from Kennedy, Kansas. Mom and Aunt Agnes are the terrors of the county. I was really young when my folks divorced. My mother and I moved back to the family farm to live with my aunt. My father was in, uh, construction. But he died a couple of years ago."

"Oh, I'm so sorry."

"Thanks. We weren't close until I was in college. Anyway, my mom's been teaching English at Kennedy High School for eons. They'll probably name the school after her someday. And Aunt Agnes is head librarian for the county."

Liza loved the way the corners of Zack's eyes crinkled when he talked about his family. She could watch his eyes for hours. They were a gorgeous shade of blue, and his eyelashes—well, wasting them on a guy was a terrible injustice.

Wait a minute! Was she on some kind of hormonal high?

"Growing up in Kennedy with Ethel and Agnes wasn't easy for a hell-raiser. They knew what I was going to do before I did it."

"They sound remarkable." Liza found herself wanting to know more about this man and his family. Not that she was interested or anything.

"They still live out on the farm. They also drive the biggest, oldest Oldsmobile 88 in the county. There isn't a funeral, wedding or baptism they don't attend. And their potato-chip-and-tuna casserole is as infamous as it is terrible."

"That's like my mother-in-law. She lives on a farm near Plains."

"I suppose once you're a farm girl, you're always a farm girl. I've tried to get them to move into town. That would certainly be more convenient, but they won't hear of it, so I gave up. You couldn't blast them out of that house." He paused to finish off his pie. "Have you ever been to Kansas?"

"I went to a conference in Kansas City. Does that count?"

"Nope, that's the big city. Kansas is the prairie. The farming communities are like oases in the wheat fields. High school activities are the center of the town's social life." He waggled his eyebrows. "Being a jock was cool. I had my pick of girls. Did you ever have a crush on an athlete?"

"Nope. Not until I met my husband."

"Since you're not wearing a ring and you're having dinner with me, I presume you're not still married."

Liza hesitated. Talking about Rob wasn't easy—and it would be even harder with the attraction she felt to Zack. But after their intense experience in the ravine, she supposed she owed it to him to be honest.

"My husband's name was Rob. He and Charlie played college basketball together. That's what I meant about the jock thing. He was tall and blond, and I was a short brunette. We weren't exactly a matched set. My daughters both take after him." She laughed. "They don't look like they ever met me."

"Do you want to tell me what happened?"

"I guess. I don't talk about this with very many people, and I'm not sure why I'm telling you, but here goes. One evening three years ago, Rob ran to the grocery store for peanut butter. He walked out the door and never came back. I'm absolutely positive that he'd never voluntarily leave us. It makes me crazy thinking about all the horrible possibilities."

Zack didn't say a word, so she continued. "Uncle Dave did an extensive search of the area and couldn't find a trace. So, now you have much more information than you probably wanted. I need another iced tea." She signaled the waitress.

Liza didn't bother to add that her fear of abandonment was so deeply rooted that she worried she might never be able to trust anyone again.

On that note, she decided she'd provided more insight into her private life than she should have, so she changed the subject.

"Why did you go to school in California?"

"My dad and his new family lived in San Francisco, so I spent part of my summers with them. Plus, he was willing to pay for my college."

"A Kansas boy turned Californian. That's quite a change."

"I suppose it is," he agreed.

Liza had been concerned about how much she'd told Zack, but he soon put her at ease. They spent the next hour talking and laughing while they shared anecdotes about Liza's daughters, Kara and Cassie, and Zack's family.

"I know this is personal, but my curiosity is getting the best of me," Liza admitted. "Are you married?"

"Nope, I've been divorced for several years. She didn't feel my job was prestigious enough."

Liza was puzzled. "Developing's not prestigious?"

"I'm not exactly a developer. In my real life, I'm a homicide detective. On leave. I got involved in a 'make my day' situation." He made finger quotes in the air. "Since I'm not working, I'm doing Kevin a favor."

"You're a policeman? No wonder you handled the shooting so well." A lot of things made sense now. "Do you really think we have a big problem?"

"I don't know. I wish I had my gun."

The most lethal weapon Liza had in her arsenal was a two-year-old can of hair spray. "I'm intrigued. What happened?"

At first he seemed hesitant to share that part of his life, but then he relented. "My partner and I were on a stakeout when this punk pulled a gun and tried to kill him. I was faster. Unfortunately, he was the nephew of a muckety-muck politician. So I was advised to take a hike until everything cooled down."

"That's too bad. How's your partner?" she asked.

"He's fine. He decided to retire. When you live on a farm outside Sacramento, people generally don't shoot at you."

Liza saw Mavis marching toward their table. "I think we've overstayed our welcome. We'd better leave her a decent tip or we won't be able to come back for fried chicken night."

She couldn't believe how much she enjoyed Zack, especially after their rocky start. A lethal situation must be the ultimate bonding experience.

"I need to get home."

"I've had fun. Next time we'll have to do this at a restaurant with tablecloths." Zack grabbed the check Mavis had left in one of her not-so-subtle attempts to get them to leave.

"I'd love that." Liza was shocked to realize she actually meant it.

Chapter Twelve

The next afternoon, Liza was in the middle of giving Zack a real-estate tutorial when Ruben stuck his head through her office door.

"Liza, I just saw Maizie at the post office. She wants you to call her. She also said that if you don't turn on your darned cell phone, she's gonna come over here and smack you. Okay, I'm outta here."

"Thanks. See you later!" she yelled as Ruben headed out the front door. "Maizie's been trying to send me on a blind date this weekend. I bet that's what this is about. I've explained over and over why I'm not interested, but so far, she refuses to give up."

Maizie was playing matchmaker for Liza. How dare she? Wait a minute! Where had that come from? Yesterday's excitement must have fried his brain. That had to be the reason the thought of her dating was so distasteful. It *couldn't* be that he was jealous.

Zack had made a solemn vow that he'd never be snookered by a woman again. Someone should tell that to his lust-o-meter. It seemed to have acquired a mind of its own.

"I'm not sure I'll learn enough of this stuff to fool anyone. I'm pretty good at B.S., but this—" he indicated the stacks of papers "—zoning stuff is wicked."

Liza laughed. "Planning's not quite as bad as homicide. And you've done really well at picking up the jargon. Let's leave it for tonight and go out for a beer."

He rubbed his temple. "I think that's a great idea."

"Gilly's is a family kind of pub."

"I'm sold. My car or yours?"

"Let's take both," she answered.

Zack didn't have a clue what she was thinking, but if her blush was any indication, she wasn't as immune to him as she pretended.

"I'm ready. How about you?" she asked, tossing papers willy-nilly into her briefcase.

Yep, he'd bet the farm he was right. She might not want to be attracted to him, but she was.

THE POPULAR PUB was crowded with early birds, so Liza pulled into the first available space. Zack found a spot half a block down and walked back to join her.

"Why is it so crowded?"

"It's the Wednesday-night church group. And there was probably a basketball game at the high school," she answered with a grin. "Small town, you know."

Zack nodded but as he stepped off the curb Liza quickly pulled him to a halt by grabbing his belt.

"Watch out!"

He jumped back as a silver Mercedes roared by, inches from where he'd been, and screeched around the corner.

"That idiot could've killed me," he fumed.

Liza couldn't help laughing.

"That idiot was my mother."

"Your mother?"

"Yes, my mother. She has a running tab with the police department for speeding tickets and parking violations. One of these days she's gonna lose her license. But until that happens, she's not giving up her car."

"Someone needs to do something. What's wrong with the cops in this place?"

"You don't have to get snotty." .

Zack seemed to realize he was sounding like a big-city, know-it-all snob. He wiped a hand down his face. "Sorry."

"I'll let you in on a little secret. She pretends she's driving a Ford. Mama takes pride in buying American."

"What about the Mercedes emblem? How can she ignore that?"

"I don't know, but she does," Liza said with a giggle. "And considering she just turned into the back parking lot, I'm guessing you're going to get the chance to meet her, up close and personal. Daddy's probably coming straight from the bank to join her. Just take everything she says with a grain of salt. Hopefully it'll be so crowded in the pub, we'll miss them."

Liza dragged him across the street and into the busy restaurant before she had a chance to change her mind. Running into her mother would undoubtedly be embarrassing. Daddy was okay, but Mama was, well…she was Mama.

"I see a table." Liza sprinted across the room to snag a recently vacated spot.

The table was so small it was difficult to move without brushing his knee with hers or touching his hand. Liza suspected he wasn't trying very hard to keep his distance. In fact, it felt as if he was scooting his chair closer and closer.

The waitress took their order and came back almost immediately with a pitcher of beer. Liza was lost in thought. Those dimples should be outlawed, not to mention that mouth! Was it possible for a guy to have a sensual mouth? *Hey, he's talking to you, stupid, so stop staring at his lips and listen up.*

"Um, I'm sorry, I drifted off. What were you saying?" Liza's flirting skills were seriously rusty.

"I asked what you felt about anchovies."

"Anchovies?" she repeated blankly. How could a girl maintain a cogent thought when a gorgeous guy was rubbing his leg against hers? And how had he managed to get that close without her noticing? She was definitely losing it, which was *not* allowed to happen. And what in the world did that have to do with anchovies?

"Hey, Liza." Much to her surprise, her father leaned over and kissed her cheek. Good heavens—while she was deep in an erotic fantasyland, her daddy had managed to sneak up on her. And where Daddy was, Mama wasn't far behind. Oh, great! She was about to get the third degree. Who was the guy? How long had she known him? Who was his family? And when were they getting married?

"Hi, Daddy. This is Zack Maynard. We're working together on the Blackwater Lake project. Zack, this is my daddy, Bennett Westerfield, and my mother, Eleanor."

Zack stood and extended his hand. "Glad to meet you, Mr. and Mrs. Westerfield. Would you like to join us?"

"Thank you, son. We have a table right over there. Mama just wanted to come by and say hey."

Uh-huh. What Mama really wanted to do was check out the guy.

"But it's right nice of you to ask. Come over to the house soon, sweetheart. We've missed you." He kissed Liza again before turning to leave. Eleanor apparently wasn't working from the same page.

"Maynard. I don't seem to recall any Maynards from around here." She sat down to launch her query. "One of my sorority sisters married a Maynard. And there are some Maynards down in Macon. Are they your people?"

"No, ma'am. My folks aren't from around here."

"Hmm."

"Come on, Eleanor. Let's leave these young people in peace." Bennett took his wife's hand and towed her across the room to their table.

"Nice guy," Zack commented.

"He's a saint to put up with Mama. She can be a pill, but I love her dearly."

Chapter Thirteen

Liza's encounter with her long-dormant libido—now alive and well—left her in a dither. Early the next morning, before she even had her first cup of coffee, Liza sent out an SOS to her twin.

"Hey, sis. I have to talk to you and Kenni—it's important." The Three Musketeers hadn't met this often since Win Whittaker had come to town and won their cousin's heart. Come to think of it, he'd arrived on a bus, too. Now *that* was interesting.

"Would you call Kenni and see if she's available? I'd do it but I'm already late for work." Liza paused before dropping the hint that would ensure her sister's attendance. "I have a plan."

"*You* have a plan?" Maizie didn't bother to disguise her good-natured sarcasm. Liza wasn't a certified planner for nothin'. She always had a plan.

"Yes, Miss Smart Mouth, I've figured out how to get Zack Maynard to leave town."

"Why would you want to do that?" Maizie asked.

"Because…" Liza couldn't verbalize the real reason, so she decided to be practical. "I can't work with him looking over my shoulder."

"Yeah, right." Maizie knew her too well.

"Why don't you come to the boutique around noon? Kenni should be free by then. I can't wait to hear this." There was only the slightest hint of a smirk in Maize's voice.

"Excellent, I'll see you then."

Liza's sexuality had been in hibernation for so long, its recent emergence was making her crazy. And every smart girl knows that's the time to head straight for the chocolate. So when Kenni breezed into the store at noon, Liza was rummaging through the cabinet looking for Maizie's secret stash.

She abandoned her search in order to give her cousin a hug. "How's life treating the newlywed?"

"Great. Absolutely fantastic! Love is where it's at."

By then Maizie had joined them and was making an elaborate show of fanning her face. "If you go into details, I'm gonna have a hot flash."

"No specifics for you." Kenni grinned as she smacked her cousin's arm. "Let's get down to business. I have a perm in an hour." Kenni McAllister Whittaker was the owner of Magnolia Bluff's premier salon. "But first, have you heard from Charlie?" she asked Liza.

"He called me last night. Darn his hide, he's in Hawaii lounging on a beach. I told him we were just peachy."

"Uh, you aren't, are you?" Maizie asked. "That's why we're meeting, isn't it?"

"No, I'm not, but Charlie doesn't need to know that." Liza frowned. "There are two things I want to talk to you guys about. One's an idea I have, and then I need some advice."

When Liza hesitated, Maizie impatiently drummed her fingernails on the table. "Get on with it," she demanded.

"Okay, here it is. Maizie, you've met Zack Maynard."

"Yes, dumbo. You know that I never, ever forget a gorgeous guy."

"Is he really *that* good-looking?" Kenni asked.

"Honey, you don't know the half of it," Maizie said, adding a lascivious wink.

Kenni grinned in acknowledgment, then switched her focus to Liza. "And?"

"And, well, I find him very attractive."

"So…?" Kenni asked.

"So, I am absolutely *not* going to get involved with him. Or anyone else for that matter. If for no other reason than the fact that legally my hands are tied. But I keep having these…uh, fantasies. You know…"

"Sugar, one of these days you're going to have to face the truth—you don't have a husband anymore. I hate to be this brutally honest, but Rob's not coming back. And we all think you should get on with living. In another year, you'll have all the legalities behind you," Maizie said, putting her arm around Liza to soften the impact of her words.

"I know, but it's so hard."

"Sweetie, I realize that. We simply want you to be happy. Don't we, Kenni?"

Kenni nodded, holding her arms open. "Group hug."

There were tears, sniffles, more hugs and a couple of *I love yous* before they untangled.

"Now back to what I was saying." Once Maizie was focused on an idea, not much could deter her.

"He's single, isn't he?"

When Liza nodded, Maizie continued. "You're both attractive. And even better, he seems like a really nice guy. So what's the problem?" She didn't wait for an answer. "Is there any chemistry? Do you feel a zing when you're around him?"

"Absolutely."

"So, I repeat, what's the problem?"

"He's a homicide cop from San Francisco, and even worse, he's butting into my business." Not really, but it sounded reasonable. "He also has an ex-wife he refuses to talk about, and that probably means he did her wrong." Actually, she was *scared* of getting involved, but too spineless to admit it. "And he's too sexy by half."

"Lordy, girl. That's a predicament? Sexy is good, sexy is wonderful," Maizie declared.

"He normally carries a gun. Do you think a guy like that would ever fit in here?"

"Are you kidding me? Half the men in this county are packing," Kenni said. Her wisdom was gained from having a husband who was a criminal defense attorney.

"Don't tell me that! There are folks in this town who don't have the sense God gave a turnip, and they might be armed?" Liza was appalled.

"Yep."

"Let's get back to the real issue," Maizie said. "You're telling me that not only does Zack have a world-class body, he also wears a gun?" She did another show of fanning herself. "I need some chocolate." She got up and dashed toward her office.

"I know you're hiding the good Belgian chocolate," Liza yelled at her retreating back. "Where is it?"

Maizie didn't answer, but in a few minutes she returned with a gold-foil-wrapped box in one hand, a truffle in the other. "Here, grab a piece. Then we can continue this conversation."

Liza and Kenni complied. They weren't dummies.

"I know you probably won't take my advice," Maizie said, nibbling on another piece of candy, "but for what it's worth, I think you need some hot, sweaty sex and darn the consequences. How many people wouldn't sell their souls for some good old-fashioned, earth-shaking lust? And if it turns out to be more, that's even better. Either way, you win."

Kenni nodded. She and her first husband had split because he'd decided he was too good to be married to a hairdresser. And the second time around she'd hit the jackpot.

"You're probably right," Liza conceded, chewing on her finger-nail. "But jeez, I don't know. Over-the-top guys are too easy to get consumed by. Rob was the world to me, and when he left I wasn't positive I'd survive." She gave a self-deprecating laugh. "In case you haven't noticed, I now have real issues about abandonment."

"Duh!" Maizie and Kenni said in unison.

"And then there's the whole matter of next year when I can have Rob declared legally dead. *That's* going to be hideous for all of us. And if—and I seriously mean *if*—I ever start dating again, it's going to be with a sensitive guy. Maybe someone who appreciates Bach."

"Get real. Bach, schmach. We're into Trace Adkins down here."

Maizie was right. Liza had been thinking the same thing. "Oh, well. Considering we've never kissed, or anything else, it's a moot point."

"Oh, really?" Maizie asked, beating Kenni to the draw.

"You know I hate it when you get smug," Liza retorted. "And don't either one of you dare breathe a word of this to Mama. Swear to goodness, if you do, I'll make your lives miserable."

"Is that any way to talk to your favorite relatives?" Maizie quickly changed the subject. "So, what's your plan?"

"Well." Liza leaned forward. "I'm almost positive the church people took down the surveyor's posts and shot poor old Linus." She figured this wasn't the right moment to tell them about the most recent episode. Thank God they hadn't heard about it through the grapevine.

"Yeah. And?" Kenni asked.

"So, I want us to stake out the place tonight. If we can catch them in action, Zack can go back to San Francisco. Then the whole sex, lust, libido problem will disappear."

"They shot a guy!" Kenni exclaimed. "I repeat, they *shot* him!"

"I know, but I suspect that Linus was in the wrong place at the wrong time. I don't think they meant to hurt him. All I want to do is see if people are wandering around the property. If they are, we can scare them off with noise. I have one of those air horns they use at football games."

Maizie stared at her sister. "You're one scary woman. I need my head examined for even considering this crazy scheme."

Kenni nodded in agreement.

"You guys will go with me, won't you?" Liza looked at

Maizie first, and then turned to Kenni. They didn't appear enthusiastic, but she was sure they'd cave. Everyone knew they were both suckers for an adventure.

"I'm in." Kenni was the first to capitulate.

"Okay, I give. Where and when?" Maizie asked.

"What are your husbands doing tonight?"

"Clayton has a Rotary meeting, and then he and the guys are going out for catfish," Maizie said.

"This is Win's first meeting, so he's going with Clayton."

"Great. We have a free evening. I'll pick you up at eight. I promise to have you home by eleven. They won't even realize you've been gone."

LIZA GLANCED AT HER REFLECTION in the cheval mirror. Not bad in an urban-guerilla kind of way. She had on Rob's old camouflage pants. They were miles too long, so she'd taken the scissors to them. Hopefully, the belt would keep them up. She was going to swelter in her black turtleneck sweater, but undercover operations required personal sacrifice. Not to mention that the long sleeves would keep the mosquitoes and no-see-ums from using her as a snack.

But the pièce de résistance was the face paint—shoe polish over a layer of Vaseline. After she applied it, she realized she should've waited until later to slather the gunk on her face.

Liza pulled into Maizie's driveway and parked behind Kenni's car. She was debating whether she should go to the front door looking like a SWAT team dropout when Maizie and Kenni emerged and jumped in the pickup.

Maizie took one glance at Liza and screeched. "Merciful heavens! Mama's right. You *are* a changeling. And what in heaven's name do you have on your face?"

"A better question is what are *you* wearing? We're heading to the woods, not to a yoga class," Liza threw back.

She'd told them to wear black, and Maizie had. It just so

happened her black ensemble consisted of a pair of spandex biker shorts and a skintight tank top.

Liza tossed Maizie the shoe polish and Vaseline. "Cover up that cleavage. Sheesh, a blind man would be able to spot you with all that white skin."

"You don't have to get snippy. You said black, and I did black. My Delta Force outfit's at the cleaners." Maizie smeared the Vaseline across her chest. "Are you sure I have to do this?"

"Yes!" Liza and Kenni said in unison.

Kenni was somewhat better at camouflage, wearing a pair of dark green cargo pants and a black T-shirt.

"I had a thought," Kenni said. "How are we going to make sure we don't get shot by your security guard?"

"Not to worry. Butter Bean McGruder's taken over as our night man. His wife, Lurleen, is in the big bowling tournament this evening. So I'm sure he's already at the Star Dust Lanes sippin' a cold one."

"Do you think the vandals know that?"

"Probably."

Liza entered a small county road that had a forest on one side and a slimy pond on the other. "We're going in the back way. When we get close enough, we'll hide the pickup and walk."

Maizie shuddered as she glanced at the murky water. "You know I can't stand snakes."

"We'll be staying on the road, so we don't have anything to worry about." At least Liza hoped they didn't. Maizie would pitch a hissy if she stepped on a timber rattler. But that really wouldn't matter, because if they so much as saw one, they'd both have a coronary.

"I'll turn off the lights so we can coast by Brother Turnipseed's trailer. I hope his dogs don't make a ruckus." Not only did Brother Turnipseed have an avid congregation of worshippers who spoke in tongues and saw visions, rumor had it he also owned a pack of coonhounds.

"I've seen that guy in town. He gives me the heebie-jeebies. And if they really do snake handling, yew!" Maizie said, then her face lit up. "Hey, that's not all bad. Maybe they've caught every last one of them."

Wouldn't that be handy?

Brother Turnipseed's compound was made up of a small concrete building and a single-wide trailer with an abandoned washing machine out front.

Liza cut the lights and rolled by without alerting a single hound. "See? We did it."

"Do you really think its Brother Turnipseed's folks doing the mischief?" Kenni asked.

"I don't know. I can't imagine who else might be involved." The folks who bought homes at Blackwater Lake were certainly going to have eccentric neighbors.

Liza parked in a stand of trees. "We can walk from here." She tossed a flashlight to each of her accomplices. "Don't use them unless you absolutely have to. I mean it. And, Maizie, no squealing." She put her hands on her hips, glaring at her best friends. "Are we ready?"

Maizie nodded reluctantly. "Even when we were kids, you got me in trouble. Everyone thought you were such an angel. Ha!"

"I got *you* in trouble?"

"Ladies, we have a job to do," Kenni said, a wicked grin on her face.

How about that? Her cousin was having fun. Naughty, naughty girl!

Chapter Fourteen

Zack settled in between two large oaks for a long stakeout. It was astonishing what a guy could buy if he knew the right place to go, and Ruben was familiar with all the shopping venues. Now Zack had the supplies he needed—a Glock 9 mm strapped to his belt, night-vision goggles, a Kevlar vest and a backup rifle. Not that he planned to shoot anyone, but it never hurt to be prepared.

He'd been watching the area for almost an hour when he saw something stir in the trees across the meadow.

"Bingo." He focused on his quarry and quickly determined that he wasn't tracking a couple of deer. The movement was too covert to be wildlife.

Sure enough, two armed men in cammies were crouched at the edge of the clearing. If his luck held, they wouldn't be toting a couple of Tech-9 assault rifles. Zack was trying to get a clear view of their weapons when out of the corner of his eye he noticed someone else in the forest. Great! He didn't need this. Two perps were plenty.

He trained the glasses on the other figures. It couldn't be— but, oh yeah, it was. The one who resembled a little kid playing war was obviously Liza. Did that woman really have mush for brains? And who were her accomplices? The Valkyrie was a no-brainer. It had to be Maizie. When Brunhilda lost her black watch cap and blond curls tumbled around her shoulders, his assumption was confirmed. The identity of the third was a puzzle. One thing was for sure—they were about to get shot, and he was the only person who could prevent it.

It took Zack half a second to decide he'd have to make himself a target. "Hey, you, what do you think you're doing out here?" he yelled.

Boom! That answered his question about the weapon. They had a shotgun. At that distance, they couldn't hit him, but the ladies were much closer, and their screeching was giving away their position.

The taller of the two trespassers turned toward them and fired.

"Liza, hit the ground!" Zack shouted, hoping to be heard over the racket.

His rifle had the range to hit the bad guys, but killing wasn't part of Zack's plan. He aimed at the trees and let off a series of shots, sending bark and dirt flying. If that didn't frighten the intruders, he didn't know what would. Fortunately, they went scurrying into the night. That was fine with him. Now he needed to deal with the escapees from the garden club.

"Stay right where you are," he yelled. "When I get over there, I want you flat on the ground, arms and legs spread." He intended to scare them.

Zack had halfway expected Liza to cut and run, but she followed orders and was prone when he approached them.

"You." He tapped Maizie's leg with his boot. "And you." He repeated the process with the third woman. "Don't move. I'm gonna strip-search this one." He lifted Liza up by her belt and put his hands under her sweater.

"Did you really think this was a good idea?" he whispered against her ear.

Liza twirled and popped him on the chest. "You jerk! You knew who we were all along. You scared the diddly-squat outta us. Jerk! Jerk! Jerk!" She punctuated each word with a smack on the arm.

Zack grabbed both her wrists until she was still. "Great outfit. But the makeup leaves a lot to be desired." He wiped the tip of her nose and her cheeks with the hem of his black T-shirt. "Gee, I guess I do know you." He turned Liza around and held her firmly, back to chest. "You can get up now, Maizie. And why don't you introduce me to your friend?"

Maizie scrambled to her feet and helped Kenni up. "This is our cousin Kenni. Kenni, this is Zack Maynard."

Zack stifled the chuckle he could feel coming on. Her introduction seemed more appropriate for a country-club luncheon than a shoot-out in the woods.

"Kenni, it's certainly nice meeting you," he said, extending his hand.

"You, too."

Liza growled. "Someone tried to kill us and you knuckleheads are practicing your Emily Post etiquette."

"And speaking of the showdown at the OK Corral." He glared at Liza, then turned his attention to Maizie. "How did she talk you into this lunacy? Those guys were armed and they meant business. What were you going to do—ask them for a donation to the church sewing guild? And do any of you have a weapon?"

"We had a plan," Liza sputtered.

"I'll bet you did. Where's your car?"

Liza waved in the direction of the pine forest.

"We'll take that into town," he said. "Tomorrow you can bring me back to retrieve the Expedition."

Zack could tell Liza didn't like his tone of voice, but in this case her options were severely limited. And she did look awfully cute in her SWAT team getup.

"There isn't enough room in my truck."

Damn! That pout was sexy!

"I guess one of you is going to have to sit on my lap." Zack couldn't help grinning from ear to ear.

Chapter Fifteen

The trip into town was as uncomfortable as a too-tight pair of jeans. When Liza pulled into Maizie's drive, her co-conspirators were out of the pickup almost before she could get stopped. Some friends they turned out to be.

"Take me back to your house, please."

At least Zack had manners.

"What do you think you're gonna do at my place?"

He leaned back against the seat and sighed. "Don't ask, just do it. I still can't believe you guys pulled a stunt like that. So humor me and drive."

"Oh, all right, but I'm starving. I guess I can feed you, too."

"It's the adrenaline."

Taking Zack home with her was a terrible idea. But Liza's common sense had apparently taken a long sabbatical. In fact, it had completely vanished about the time *he'd* shown up.

She lived almost a mile out of town in a restored farmhouse. It was her refuge, and she didn't know whether she was willing to share it with a stranger—not even one as appealing as Zack Maynard. Or maybe that was the problem.

"I'm not sure if I could find this place again," Zack mused, eyeing the forest that bordered the road. "What's all that vine-looking stuff? It seems to be everywhere."

"That's kudzu. It's invasive and nobody knows how to get rid of it. It covers up a multitude of sins, like abandoned cars and old sofas. They're planning to widen this road. No telling what they'll find."

"Interesting."

"Yep. Here we are." Liza turned onto a gravel drive. Several hundred yards down the road, the woods opened into a meadow.

"The house is called Belle Meade." She used a remote control to open a large metal gate. The rambling white clapboard house with green shutters and wraparound porch was typically Southern. A trellised grape arbor adorned the detached garage. Flowering azaleas and camellias surrounded the house, creating the impression of icing on a wedding cake.

"I have a front door, but I don't remember the last time anyone used it." In the South, the only people who came in the front door were salesmen and preachers.

Liza knew she wasn't fooling Zack with her delaying tactics. She was keeping up the chitchat so he wouldn't be able to chew her out.

Zack followed her in the back door and took a look around. "In houses this old, you expect to find a lot of small rooms, but this—" he waved at the single living area showcasing an ornate fireplace on the waterside of the house "—is spectacular."

He was making civilized conversation. Was that good or bad? Liza couldn't decide. Maybe it was a cop thing, but whatever it was, she could play along.

"When I moved in, there were four separate rooms on this floor. I had two parlors and a formal dining room. As you can see, I left the main entrance and tore down most of the other walls. I wanted an open look. It's been a three-year project, but I think I'm finally finished," Liza said with pride. "When I couldn't sleep, I'd grab my sander." She laughed at the memory. "As you can see, I had a problem with insomnia."

He didn't have an opportunity to respond before P.B. bounded down the stairs, and slid to a stop. Leaning against Zack's legs, he lolled his head back and waited to be petted.

"You know P.B., but you haven't met Jelly Belly." Liza indicated a tiny black toy poodle sitting beside the golden. "She's as silly as he is. I'll bet anything they were napping upstairs on the guest bed.

"Were you being naughty?" Liza asked as she bent over to rub a curly black ear. "Jelly is a poodle," she whispered. "But we don't say that out loud. She thinks she's a big dog."

"Okay, how are you, Bruiser?" Zack asked in a deep baritone.

"You'd better watch out or Jelly's gonna fall in love with you," Liza warned him. "Come on, guys, dinner's ready." She headed to the laundry room with the dogs trotting along behind her. "I need to take care of them before I can do anything else."

She suggested Zack wait for her in the kitchen.

"I think there's a bottle of Chardonnay in the fridge if you like white. There's probably a red in the wine rack, and the corkscrew's in the drawer next to the pantry." Liza hoped he could hear her over the loud chomping noises and the sound of plastic bowls scraping across the tile floor.

Zack was leaning against the countertop with his booted feet crossed when Liza finished her doggy chores.

"I also have to feed the horses. If you want to open the wine, I'll be right back. The boys usually do this, but they went to Atlanta with their mom. I'll bet those poor animals are starving."

He took her arm. "Before you do that, let me get rid of some of that face paint." He wet a paper towel at the sink and took her chin in his hand. "I'm not sure I want to drink wine with a female Rambo." He gently dabbed at the shoe polish. He pushed a lock of hair behind her ear and ran a fingertip down the side of her cheek. It was a simple act, but so sensual she almost had a heart attack.

And there were those dimples again. Oh, wow! Why was it so hard to breath?

"Do you mind if I help you with the horses?" he asked.

Did she mind if he did anything? No, no and no. She'd have given him the deed to the house if he'd asked.

Liza was surprised her voice didn't come out as a squeak. "Not at all. We'll make a country boy out of you yet."

"I grew up on a farm, remember?"

"Oh yeah, I forgot. You *are* a country boy. You don't look like one." She gave him a once-over and waggled her eyebrows. She had to lighten this up or she might end up in an untenable position. So to speak…

"Do you also listen to Garth Brooks and Trisha Yearwood?" she asked.

"You betcha. I'm a good old boy at heart." And to prove it, he ambled toward the barn.

The two-story barn stood like a sentinel over the pastures. Liza opened the big double doors and flipped on the lights, dispelling the gloom. She stopped in a room filled with feed sacks, saddles and assorted horse tack. Grabbing a metal bucket, a handful of feed and two halters, she returned to the main aisle and handed one of the halters to Zack.

He shook it, making it jingle. "I assumed your grandchildren were babies, but I was obviously wrong. Even prodigies don't play soccer and ride horses." How could this sexy, alluring woman have school-age grandchildren? She barely looked old enough to drink.

Liza laughed as she scooped out the grain. "They're actually my step-grandchildren. Cassie's husband has two boys from his first marriage. My daughter's only twenty-three."

"That's awfully young to be responsible for two children."

"Isn't that the truth? But she's doing a wonderful job, and I adore the rascals. Let's go find us some ponies." Liza did a really bad John Wayne impression. "Let me warn you, the little buggers can be downright devious." She turned on the outside lights and led the way to the pasture.

The noise of feed rattling in the metal bucket immediately got the attention of the horses grazing at the back of the field. The black pony eyed the humans disdainfully, but hunger finally won out. The larger white one continued to graze, periodically glancing at the feed bucket and his friend. Curiosity and an empty stomach eventually took their toll, and he strolled over, too.

Liza gave a slight tug on the lead rope, providing encouragement enough for the pony to follow her to the barn. Zack did the same with his captive.

"Snowflake goes on the right." Liza gestured toward an empty stall. "The water hose is in the aisle. You can fill their buckets while I finish getting their grain and hay. The kids cleaned the stalls this morning, so we can skip that part."

They worked companionably, quickly finishing the task and returning to the house.

"The powder room is down the hall on the left. Everything you'll need is in there. I'm going to change and wash up." Jelly Belly pranced behind her up the stairs, while P.B. followed Zack to the small bathroom. Zack shut the door in his adoring, slobbery face.

His canine friend was still blocking the door when he finished washing, so Zack hopped over him and went in search of the wine. He retrieved two glasses from the cabinet and found the unopened Chardonnay in the refrigerator. Angela had always made fun of the fact he didn't know a merlot from a shiraz. Did he really care? He was a Budweiser kind of guy.

Zack took his wineglass and wandered into the living area where two overstuffed couches flanked a blue-and-coral silk rug. He didn't know much about interior design, but he recognized comfortable, and this room was exactly that. It was the antithesis of the house he'd shared with Angela, which had all the comfort of a modern-art museum.

He saw an entertainment center near the fireplace. CDs had to be close at hand. He rifled through the pile of discs and found an eclectic mix of country-western, vintage seventies, classical and R and B. He flipped an Elton John into the player.

"I like that music," Liza commented when she joined him. "It's soothing, and after tonight, I appreciate tranquil."

She was beautiful in an all-natural way. This woman in her baggy cotton pants and oversize UGA T-shirt was the real thing. She was gorgeous right down to the bottom of her soul.

And that scared the heck out of him!

Chapter Sixteen

Zack was a master at multitasking, so as he poured Liza a glass of wine he gave himself a mental bop on the noggin. The timing was terrible. After Angela, he'd sworn off women. Yeah, tell that to his...his whatever.

"Did you go to the University of Georgia?" What a dumb question. But it was the best he could·come up with when all he wanted to do was lay her down on the couch and have his way with her. That would really be stupid—delectable, but stupid.

"No, actually, I didn't." She looked down at the logo on the shirt. "I went to Georgia Tech, UGA's archenemy. My under-graduate degree was in land-use planning. But Maizie went to UGA. She even pledged a sorority. According to Mama, she's the good daughter."

"Why's that?"

"Because she knows what to do with a finger bowl," Liza said with a laugh.

"That's an interesting criteria."

"My thought, too. Why don't you come with me to the kitchen and keep me company while I cook."

"Yes, ma'am."

"How does a chicken stir-fry sound?" She retrieved the meat and vegetables from the refrigerator and dropped them on the butcher block.

"Home cooking sounds like heaven. Can I help?" Zack secretly hoped she'd say no. That way he could continue to observe her.

"No. Just sit down and relax. I love to have someone to talk to while I cook." She pointed at the two dogs napping by his feet. "They're not much for conversation. You can set the table, if you'd like. We'll eat in the breakfast room." She indicated a glass extension of the kitchen that resembled a tropical rain forest.

Like most guys he knew, Zack was out of his element when it came to houseplants. Too much water, too little water—regardless of what he did, they always seemed to die. He figured that was the reason God made silk plants.

"You like greenery, huh?" Again with the inane conversation!

"I suppose I got carried away." Liza continued to chop vegetables. "I like to have as much sun as possible. The house already had several floor-to-ceiling windows, but I added more. If I didn't live so far out in the country, I wouldn't be able to run around naked."

He didn't think her remark was funny. Just the thought of her cavorting about the living room naked as the day she was born was disturbing in more ways than one. First of all, there were crazies running around. And second, it fostered some incredibly R-rated fantasies.

Working on the assumption that a confrontation would cure what ailed him, Zack broached the topic they'd both been avoiding.

"So, what were you planning to do out on the job site dressed like Chuck Norris?"

HE WANTED TO FIGHT? That was too bad. Kissing would be a whole lot more fun. "Not that it's any of your business, but we decided to find out who's been sabotaging us."

He leaned down until they were nose to nose. "What were you going to do when you caught them? Immobilize them with hair spray?"

That was darned close. And now that he'd said it out loud, it sounded pathetic. But he didn't need to know that. "I had a strategy."

"I'll bet you did." He was staring at her lips like he wanted to kiss her.

What she wouldn't give for a taste, just one slow, luscious taste.

He shook his head as if to clear his senses. "Isn't it about time we did this?" He bent lower and closed the small gap between them.

She had the weirdest feeling in her tummy. Was she getting an ulcer? When the kiss turned into a full-fledged lip-lock, Liza knew she was in a world of trouble. He smelled woodsy, clean and male. Now *that* was a dangerous combination.

When he slipped a hand under her sweatshirt, Liza fought the urge to purr. She felt like a cat in a field of catnip, or a shopping addict at an after-Christmas sale. How could a girl think when he was caressing the soft skin of her midriff?

He didn't seem to need any encouragement, but Liza knew a great thing when she felt it, so she went after his delicious mouth with a vengeance. She kissed one dimple and then the other, his earlobe and that sensual—oh, wow—sexy lower lip.

"Earth to Liza." Although she realized he was talking to her, he could have been speaking Swahili.

"We have to quit while I'm still able to," he croaked.

She burrowed deeper into his neck. All thoughts of being responsible or sensible had gone AWOL.

He chuckled, but didn't push her away. "I'm definitely not prepared."

"You feel prepared to me," she murmured, pressing herself against him.

He winced as he readjusted her body. "I'm not ready, you know, as in Trojans." He looked down at his lap.

"Oh, my gracious!" She blushed right to the roots of her hair. Protection hadn't entered her mind.

He lowered her sweatshirt and stroked her cheek. "You're really cute when you get all red."

"Carmine," she whispered.

"Oh, yeah, I forgot." He pulled her against his chest. "You don't use regular color names." He kissed the top of her head. "I won't be caught unprepared again. In fact, I'm going straight to the drugstore to buy the party pack. We're not finished with this, not by a long shot."

Liza couldn't decide whether that was a threat or a promise. Both sounded scary.

"I've decided to run into Atlanta in the next couple of days to hire some additional security. Why don't you come with me?"

How could he discuss business when all she wanted to do was get him naked? Men! They had everything going for them. They peed standing up, they never had insomnia, and to top it all off, they could *compartmentalize*. It was totally unfair.

She sighed, attempting to get her head on straight. Focusing on work accomplished that.

"I'd like go to Atlanta with you, but we have a meeting with the county planning folks tomorrow. We have big problems. Lost applications, employee changes, you name it and they've done it. I suspect we're being sabotaged. Perhaps after you meet the committee, you can figure out what's happening."

"I'll do my best." He kissed her one last time. "I'm leaving now, so turn on the alarm and *don't* parade around naked."

"Yes, sir." She tried to suppress her giggle, to no avail.

Liza watched Zack's car disappear down the driveway. What in the world had just happened? She looked toward the water, and the hair on the back of her neck stood at attention. She had the creepiest feeling someone was watching her.

Chapter Seventeen

Bright and early the next morning, Zack joined Liza and Ruben at the office for a briefing on the upcoming meeting. He was supposed to be thinking about the project, but in truth, he was distracted by the radical change in his professional focus and the confusing shift in his personal life.

Zack was an expert at police work. However, when it came to real-estate development, he was a neophyte. Combine that with the fact that he had the hots for a sexy grandmother and you had one heck of a sticky situation.

"I wonder what Zack's going to make of the planning department's resident dominatrix?" Ruben asked, strolling to the coffeepot for a refill. "Have you warned him?"

"I thought I'd surprise him, but perhaps I should give him a heads-up." A sly grin crossed Liza's face. "Who knows, maybe she's his type."

This conversation did not sound encouraging. "What are you guys talking about?"

If Ruben's smirk was any indication, Zack wasn't going to like the answer.

"Let's just say the planner responsible for our project has been called a… Hmm, what would be a charitable description, Liza?"

"Tramp, slut. Take your pick."

Ruben tweaked her nose. "Aw, come on, Liza, don't mince words."

"How about a cross between Attila the Hun and Gypsy Rose Lee?"

Zack joined in the banter. "Sounds like a couple of cross-dressers I ran across in San Francisco. Would you like to hear about them?"

"No, thanks, I'll pass." Liza picked up her briefcase. "I told the engineers to meet us at the courthouse, so we'd better get rolling. Ruben, grab the presentation boards." She gave Zack a saucy wink.

"Got your whip ready?" she asked.

THE BUILDING THAT HOUSED the planning and public works departments reminded Zack of his precinct digs—drab, nondescript and ugly. But even prison guards had more fashion sense than the slightly pudgy, middle-aged woman at the reception desk.

"Can I help you?" she drawled.

Zack wondered whether he'd ever get used to the way Southerners could turn a single syllable into three.

Ruben strolled up to the desk with a grin. "Hey, Lucy, how's old Bubba doin'?" He leaned against the counter, ready for a chat-up.

"Well, his favorite coonhound got out and now she's havin' a litter by that scruffy mutt next door, but other than that he's doin' right fine. Our big worry is that Danny Bob's about to get kicked out of Mississippi State. But you don't want to hear my troubles. You here for a meeting?"

"Yep, we have an appointment with Bambi and the gang. Are they ready?"

She made a production of checking her schedule. "I'll tell them you're here. Go on back to the Magnolia room. You know where it is, don't you?"

"Sure thing." Without missing a beat, Ruben sauntered through the doors marked Authorized Personnel Only, motioning for Zack and Liza to follow.

"What did she mean that we're in the Magnolia room?" Zack asked.

Ruben gave him what Zack was beginning to recognize as his *I know this is stupid, but what can you do?* look.

"A couple of years ago the Board of Supervisors decided to redo the place. So they named the conference rooms for local vegetation. They used names like the Mimosa and the Magnolia. You know you've hit rock bottom when they send you to the Kudzu room."

"The whole thing's so ridiculous it had to be G. Harry's idea," Liza said, leading the way toward a conference room.

It could've passed for an *NYPD Blue* set—austere, poorly decorated and depressing. The politicos certainly hadn't spent any of the taxpayers' money on frivolous items like comfortable furniture and accent lighting. Straight-back metal chairs with aging red fabric surrounded a long gray table.

"I thought you said they redecorated."

Ruben pointed at a framed photo of a tree. "Check it out. You should have seen it before they added the pictures."

While Liza was assembling the presentation, an array of planners, engineers and managers joined them in the stark room.

"Where are Trevor and Bambi?" Liza asked, then turned her attention to Zack. "Trevor is the planning director," she explained.

The missing participants were already fifteen minutes late, and counting. Zack mentally moved the two tardy staff members to the top of his list for background checks.

Another ten minutes passed before a distinguished-looking man with steel-gray hair joined the meeting. "I'm Trevor Creekmore, the planning director. Bambi will be here in a few minutes. I apologize. She's frequently tardy."

That was like the pot calling the kettle black.

When Bambi finally deigned to appear, Zack was poleaxed. The woman was an Amazon! She had to be at least six foot one in her stocking feet, and with the red stiletto heels, she soared into the stratosphere. He'd never seen legs quite that long, or a skirt that short.

He tried—honestly he did—but he couldn't keep from trailing his eyes up her body to cleavage that was barely restrained by a fuzzy pink sweater. An astonishing swath of blue eye shadow and a towering beehive of teased bleached-blond hair completed the picture. Zack could feel, rather than hear, Ruben laughing.

"Hi, I'm Bambi, with an *I*," the woman gushed as she rounded the table and poked her red talons in his face.

It took a moment for his manners to take hold, but when they did, he stood. "I'm Zack Maynard."

"See, a gentleman stands when a lady enters the room." She taunted the men on the other side of the table. "Trevor, you want to get this meeting started or do you want me to take it?"

"Go ahead, Bambi, it's your show."

"THAT WENT WELL ENOUGH. What do you think of Inga the Norse raider?" Ruben thumped Zack on the back. "Wait till you see her in action. She and Sam Coleson work in tandem. Unfortunately, they frequently place such onerous conditions on a development, the project simply goes away."

Liza pushed open the door to the parking lot. "I've seen it happen more than once," she concurred.

Ruben was half a step behind her. "Occasionally they deal well with the developer, but sometimes they don't. I hope Trevor Creekmore keeps an eye on things, at least until we get through the political stuff."

"Which one was Sam Coleson?" Zack asked.

"He's the senior inspector, short, chubby, wire-rimmed glasses," Liza said. "He seems pretty innocuous, but I've heard some rumors. Guess we'll wait and see what happens."

"What kind of rumors?"

"Vague stuff. Hints about bribes. But you know how that goes. The gossip could have been started by someone who didn't like a decision he made." Liza shrugged. "Oh, by the way, Leonard Dunwoodie called. He's on the Board of Supervisors. He said he could see us this afternoon at four-thirty, so I agreed. I hope that's convenient for you."

"Four-thirty is fine," Zack replied. "That'll give me time to check in with the main office."

THE POLITICIAN'S DESK WAS littered with dirty coffee cups and stacks of manila folders when Liza and Zack arrived that afternoon. Leonard was already seated at a round conference table chomping on a handful of gumdrops.

"Come in, come in," he directed. "Have some candy. I've heard a lot about you." He stood and pumped Zack's hand. "I have some questions."

But instead of asking anything, he launched into a monologue. "I think we need to admit we aren't providing even basic services to some parts of this county, especially the folks who live out near Blackwater Lake. And your project can provide money for the infrastructure we need." Leonard popped another handful of gumdrops in his mouth.

"As long as you keep to the parameters you outlined, and cough up the financial help we need, you can count on my support." Leonard continued to speak, not allowing Zack or Liza more than a nod. "You know you need to get the department heads on your team, don't you?" The question was obviously rhetorical. "Just keep me informed. And good luck. You're gonna need it. Now, I have to get home or my wife's going to be put out." He walked them to the door, chatting the entire time.

"What did you think of the meeting?" Liza asked as she and Zack strolled across the parking lot to the Expedition.

Zack hit the car's keyless entry. "He certainly likes to talk."

"No kidding. But I do think he's on our side."

"How about the other two?" Zack asked.

"If I was guessing, I'd have to say G. Harry's going to be a hard nut to crack, but I've been wrong before. We need two out of three, and I think Helen's our best bet," Liza said.

"You're the expert." Zack helped Liza into the truck before jogging around to the driver's side. After he jumped in, he glanced at his passenger.

"I don't want to eat alone. Could I talk you into having dinner with me?"

Liza thought for a few seconds. It was Mama's sewing circle night, so they were more than likely safe from an ambush.

"Sure. There's a good barbecue place out by the county line." No use taking a chance on another third degree from Mama. Not that she could avoid it for long. Magnolia Bluffs was a very small town, and it had an incredibly active rumor mill.

Chapter Eighteen

"Elizabeth, wait a minute, dear." Liza heard Mama's voice from the other side of the Piggly Wiggly produce section, but an interrogation across a bin of cabbage *wasn't* her idea of a good time.

Uh-oh! Her mother barreled past a sale on fresh peaches without even a sidelong glance. Mama was one of the original black-belt shoppers, so if she passed up peaches for forty-nine cents a pound, she was a woman on a mission.

Liza pulled her cart over. "Hi, Mama." She waited for an air kiss.

Leave it to Eleanor Westerfield to take on the grocery store in a classic shirtwaist dress, tasteful pumps and, of course, her pearls. She was a twenty-first-century June Cleaver.

After dispensing a hug and a kiss, she got down to business. "Why haven't you brought that young man to the house for dinner?"

"We've been really busy. And besides, he's simply a colleague." Lying was such a pain. "Did I tell you he's from San Francisco?" *That* should stop her in her tracks.

"San Francisco. You mean California? Oh, goodness!" Eleanor looked a bit green around the gills. "Well, never mind. We still need to have him to dinner. Sunday. I'll make my special chicken and dumplings."

"I'll ask him and let you know." Sure.

"Have you heard from Charlie?" Liza's business partner was one of Eleanor's favorite people.

"Yes," Liza said with a smile. "Darn his hide, he's in Mexico swilling drinks. The man is traveling so much I can't keep track of him, but I got the impression he might be coming home."

Mama turned serious. "I know there haven't been any kidnappings in a while, but I'm still concerned about you."

As vexing as her mother could be, she meant well. She just had a few quirks. "I'll be fine. Honest." She didn't bother to mention the latest shooting .

Her mother didn't look convinced.

"What *are* you wearing?" Eleanor asked in a quick non sequitur.

Liza glanced down at her red cotton overalls. "Overalls?"

"That's probably why you weren't able to pledge Kappa Delta Theta like Maizie."

Not again! "I didn't want to be in Kappa Delta Theta. I'm not even sure that Tech had Kappa Delta Theta. May I also add I didn't want to be in the Dixie Belles back in high school? Maizie was the one who went for the girlie stuff, not me."

"Oh, well, never mind. Be sure to invite your young man to dinner."

Liza hugged her mother. "Okay. I'll ask him. Now, I've got to run. I have stuff to do at the office." With the speed of a NASCAR driver, she wheeled her cart out of the produce section.

LIZA WAS STARING BLANKLY at her computer screen when the telephone jangled, breaking her concentration—or what little she had. Nowadays, the only thing she could think about was the guy with those annoying dimples and that world-class rear.

"Liza Henderson."

It was Maizie, and she was in full take-charge mode. "You remember we're going to the shower for Vivian this evening, don't you?"

No, Liza had erased that bit of information. The whole pink wedding, pink bridal shower and pink hoopskirt ordeal was so over-the-top she couldn't believe she'd agreed to take part in any of it.

"Yes, I remember." Liar, liar, pants on fire!

"You'd better, 'cause if you don't show up at Miz Pierpoint's house after I RSVP'd for you, you'll never get invited to another event in Magnolia Bluffs as long as you live." Camille Pierpoint was the queen-bee social diva of Magnolia Bluffs and its environs. An invitation to her house was on par with a command appearance at Buckingham Palace. And a whole lot more intimidating.

"Don't forget, it's a pink tea."

Liza uttered an expletive. "I don't have a single solitary pink thing in my closet."

"Go buy something. Vivian matched everything—the flowers, our dresses, the napkins, *everything*—to Miz Pierpoint's mother's favorite china. You absolutely *have* to wear pink."

"Okay, okay, don't get all riled up." For a brief second, Liza considered picking up an obnoxious pink rag at the dollar store. Although the fantasy was appealing, she knew she'd buy something tasteful and more than likely expensive.

PIERPOINT MANOR WAS THE OLDEST and most elegant house in Magnolia Bluffs. Built well before the Civil War, the venerable mansion exuded Southern aristocracy and family money. Camille Pierpoint, on the other hand, oozed thirty-year-old Scotch and French perfume.

Liza gritted her teeth and started through the receiving line. "Miz Pierpoint. It's nice to see you again."

The grande dame patted her hand and pinched her cheek. "Liza Henderson. Don't you look cute and perky in your pink?"

Before she could respond, Maizie pushed her along. It was probably just as well. Anything she said would have shocked the socks off the Junior Leaguer ahead of them.

"Cousin Vivian, you're as pretty as a picture." Maizie air kissed their relative.

This was Vivian's fourth trip to the altar, and she had more deviled-egg dishes than she could use in a lifetime. Her previous marriages weren't an accepted topic of conversation. Neither was Liza's opinion that husband number four was the biggest nerd in Georgia—maybe even the entire South. He was nice, but he was still geeky.

His assets included a very healthy portfolio, ancestry dating back to the Revolutionary War and a bright political future. If he made Vivian happy, Liza was as pleased as punch. She just wished she could be more of an observer and less of a contributor to the festivities.

Vivian burst into tears as she enveloped Liza in a hug. "Liza, Maizie, I'm glad you came. I'm an emotional wreck when I get married." Although Vivian was also forty-four, she hadn't changed much since high school. Give the girl a couple of pom-poms and a short skirt, and she could probably still make the cheer squad.

"You know Cordell's cousin, Helen Damon, don't you?" Vivian asked, but before Liza could answer, Vivian turned to the politician. "Hard to believe Liza and Maizie are twins, isn't it?"

Out of her Birkenstocks, Board of Supervisors member Helen Damon was a different woman. Especially when her face was an alarming shade of fuchsia that coordinated nicely with her hot-pink suit.

Helen whipped a battery-operated fan out of her purse and pointed it at her face. "Don't mind me. It's the menopause. Sometimes I think I'm dying. Then others, I'm absolutely positive I'm terminal. You know, I had a twin, but I lost him years ago."

Liza couldn't imagine being without Maizie. They shared everything except clothes, and had done so all their lives. It was a bond that was unbreakable.

"I'm sorry. That's terrible."

Helen waved a hand in a gesture of dismissal. "It was a long time ago."

A few hours later, they were done. Liza had survived the bridal shower. Hip, hip, hooray—only a couple dozen social functions to go!

Chapter Nineteen

The next day Liza leaned against the doorjamb of Ruben's office and spoke in the syrupy sweet voice she used when she needed a *really big* favor.

"Ruben, would you call G. Harry and set up a meeting? Pretty please? I'd do it, but I don't want to talk to him on the phone, or anywhere else."

Ruben's irritating smirk told her he wasn't going to make this easy.

"Um, would you also *go* to the meeting for me?" she asked.

Liza went all the way into the office and flopped on the couch. "The man's always trying to touch me. It's enough to gag a maggot."

Ruben leaned back in his leather desk chair and smiled. "I know some gossip. Want to hear it?"

Liza propped her feet on the coffee table. "Are you kidding?"

"You've heard about G. Harry and the porn?"

"Certainly."

"According to my snitch, he spends hours on the Internet. And he issues strict orders not to be disturbed unless the place is burning down," Ruben said with a chuckle. "Dollars to dough-nuts, he's not checking the weather report."

Liza responded with an unladylike snort.

"G. Harry's peccadilloes are the talk of the entire staff. And here's the *really* good news. I think someone's about to narc on him." Ruben's chuckle blossomed into a full-blown guffaw.

"Fabulous. Hopefully he'll get his."

"But back to the business at hand. I'll be glad to call him. He doesn't have any lascivious interest in me." Ruben continued to laugh, but then got serious. "Why don't you deck him when he tries something?"

Actually that wasn't a bad idea. "Okay, when he mentions the Pine Tree Motel, I'll smack him into the next time zone. What do you think?"

"Go for it, girl."

"On to a more pleasant topic," Liza segued. "I set up a meeting with Helen. I also had a very productive talk with some of the other staff members yesterday. I think most of them are supporting us."

"That's what I like to hear. Want a goodie?" Ruben indicated the loaf of banana bread wrapped in aluminum foil.

"Sure. Who did the baking?"

"Yvonne."

"That's good. For a minute there, I was afraid you'd taken up cooking."

"Ha, ha."

Liza cut a piece. "What do you know about Helen?"

"Not much. Only what's fairly common knowledge. Helen grew up in Atlanta. She didn't move here until she was in her thirties. She started her political career doing volunteer work and moved on from there."

"That's interesting. I hadn't heard any of that."

"I think Helen's okay. She has her quirks, but we can work around them," Ruben said. "On that note, I'll call the nuttiest of the nuts." Liza didn't want to hear any of that conversation, so she retreated to her office.

She sat at her desk, staring at the pile of papers. Lord help her, she was having prurient thoughts—lustful fantasies of whipped cream and rumpled sheets. And when the man she'd cast in those daydreams stuck his head in the door, she nearly swallowed her tongue.

"We have an appointment with Helen Damon for lunch tomorrow, if it's all right with you," she squeaked, then cleared her throat. "She's on the board of supervisors, remember?" *Stop the babbling.* "Anyway, we're supposed to meet her at the gazebo in the park, if it's a nice day." Good heavens! It was always a nice day in April, except when they had a thunderstorm, and those usually didn't happen until afternoon. Now she was mentally babbling. "If it rains, we'll meet her at the Daisy. It's a vegetarian restaurant."

"Okay." Zack gave her a strange look before wandering off toward the kitchen.

Maybe he hadn't noticed that she'd suddenly turned into the village idiot. Liza took a deep breath. It was impossible to think when he was around. Unfortunately, her reprieve was short-lived as Zack returned from the kitchen and let himself into her office.

"Ruben just told me that he set up the meeting with G. Harry. He also explained why you're hesitant to go with us." Zack sat down in the chair across from her desk. "If you want, I'll have a little talk with him." He said it so quietly that it took a few seconds to register.

"What do you mean, 'a little talk'?"

Zack grinned. "Oh, you know. Nothing serious, just scare the crap out of him, shoot him, that kind of thing."

"No!"

"Okay, if you insist," he said. "I don't want you to do anything that makes you uncomfortable, especially for the benefit of Blackwater." He smacked his hand on the desk. "I'm planning to do a thorough check on those supervisor yahoos, and G. Harry's gonna be right at the top of that list. If he's ever spit on the sidewalk, I'll find out. I wonder why no one's filed a sexual harassment on him."

That was easy. "They'd lose their job if they complained."

They were still discussing the inequity of the situation when Ruben joined them.

Zack crossed one foot over his leg. "I was just offering to castrate G. Harry. What do you think?"

"That's the best idea I've heard in a long time," Ruben agreed. "Wait until after we get his vote, then I'll help you."

Chapter Twenty

Zack parked the Expedition at the town's historic depot, and he and Liza ambled to the gazebo. Due to the heat and humidity, ambling—or moseying, or whatever you wanted to call it—was the standard form of locomotion all over the South. Speed was not an option.

Lacy wisteria draped the latticed gazebo in an explosion of purple. The crepe myrtle and azaleas surrounding the structure proudly displayed translucent flowers that ranged in color from magenta to petal-pink to white.

"During the Fourth of July celebration, this area is used for band concerts. We have an old-fashioned Fourth with picnicking on the grass, music, kids, dogs, the whole bit. Do you think you'll be around until then?"

Probably not, as long as he could straighten out his professional life. All the same, the thought of sticking around was starting to have a lot of appeal. "Uh, I don't know."

Liza gave him an indecipherable look. His hesitation was obviously not lost on her.

"Helen's here already." She indicated a woman unpacking a large picnic basket.

The politician was exactly what he'd expected—a typical 1970s earth mother with frizzy gray hair ruthlessly scraped back in a bun and no makeup. The hippie look was emphasized by her

Birkenstocks, flowing cotton print skirt and elaborately beaded vest. She was somewhere between forty and sixty, and from what Liza had told him, she was an ardent environmentalist.

"Hi, Helen. I don't believe you've met Zack Maynard."

The politician smiled warmly. "I've heard a lot about you. Please sit down. I've made us some lunch." There was an elaborate spread of sandwiches, an enormous fruit salad and a mountain of cookies. "I hope you like egg salad. I'm a vegan, but I won't impose that on you. Some vegans can be such toads." She laughed as she set out plates, napkins and silverware.

"I've heard you made quite an impression on the planning and public works staff. That's definitely an accomplishment. I've also talked to several of the department managers and they all seem to be impressed with your project. And of course, I've also spoken to Bambi." Helen wrinkled her nose in distaste. "I'll tell you this in confidence. I'm not impressed with that girl. I suppose she's a hard worker. But…" She left the rest of her thought unsaid.

"We brought some schematics to show you. We can roll them out after we eat and answer any questions you might have," Liza said. "Is this iced tea?" She pointed to a large frosty jar filled with amber liquid.

"Peach herbal. I hope you don't mind that it's not the normal stuff. I'm not into caffeine. So, lunch is ready—dig in? I'll be very insulted if you leave a crumb," she teased.

They spent almost two hours discussing the project. "I'm really glad we had this meeting," Helen said, repacking the picnic basket. "Now I don't have to rely on secondhand information. But I'm sure I'll have some questions. If I do, I'll call you."

"Certainly." Zack handed her his card, then picked up the picnic basket to carry it to her car.

Liza and Zack watched as Helen drove away in a battered green Volkswagen bus. "I can't believe she has Grateful Dead stickers on her van," Liza said.

Wasn't that the truth? "How do you think that went?" Zack asked as he hit the remote lock on the Expedition.

"Pretty well, other than the fact you grimaced whenever she patted your hand and called you 'young man,'" Liza said. "She must think you're awfully young."

"She sees herself as very maternal. I suspect that anyone under sixty is a kid to her. Actually, I think it was productive," he said.

"I do, too."

Zack hated to broach an unpleasant subject, especially when they were having a good time, but he felt compelled to ask. "Did you realize that our meeting with G. Harry is tomorrow morning?"

Liza made loud, kissy noises. "Send him my love."

ZACK DROVE LIZA BACK to her office to retrieve her old pickup.

"Will you be okay driving that thing home, or do you want me to follow you?" He didn't trust the truck Liza lovingly called Oscar. "And why are you driving the jalopy?" After his initial Clampett experience, Zack had discovered that Liza's usual mode of transportation was a bit more upscale. And best of all, it wasn't held together with spit and a prayer.

"I had to run by the feed store to pick up some chow for the animals. Don't worry." She patted his arm. "Oscar's trustworthy."

Zack could tell she was lying, but he couldn't do anything about it.

"That girl needs a keeper," he muttered as he watched her wrestle the wheezing, coughing heap down the road.

THE COUNTRY LANE TO LIZA'S house ran through a forested wetland that was home to hundreds, if not thousands, of water moccasins. When Liza drove Oscar, she always tuned in to the local country-western station. Trace Adkins, Martina McBride and Oscar—it all seemed to fit.

She was humming along with Martina when she glanced in

her rearview mirror and noticed a small car sucking up to her tailpipe. The windows were so heavily tinted she couldn't see the driver.

If that didn't beat all! Liza maintained her speed, but the knucklehead slammed against her rear bumper. He was trying to force her off the road! She grabbed the steering wheel in a death grip. There was no way she was spending the night with a bunch of reptiles.

The second time he smashed into the truck, it jarred her teeth right to her molars. *Okay, think. What would Lara Croft do?*

There was a small verge a couple of hundred feet down the road. If she could make it that far, she could whip off and he'd be forced to go by. If she was lucky, and skilled and…

As she approached the verge, Liza seized the opportunity by yanking the steering wheel and slamming on her brakes. She'd just breathed a sigh of relief when the damned idiot made a 180 and angled in front of her truck.

A second car pulled up behind her, effectively trapping her. Now that rated a big C-R-A-P! *Come on, Lara, how about a little inspiration?* Liza hit the door locks, not that she really thought the flimsy things would offer much protection if the scumbags truly wanted to hurt to her. What she wouldn't give for a shiny .22. Instead she was going to have to make do with an out-of-date can of pepper spray and a cell phone.

She started to dial 911—not that she believed Booty or any of his buddies would make it in time—when the driver of the front car gunned the engine and peeled out. The second vehicle quickly followed.

When she spotted Ron Harkins in his fire marshal's Blazer she realized what had happened. The emergency lights on his truck had spooked them. Liza wanted to jump out and kiss him, but she was afraid her legs wouldn't hold her up.

Ron strolled up to her window. "Hey, Liza, what's happening? Do you need some help?"

She dropped her head on the steering wheel. The adrenaline was slowly subsiding, and she felt weak. She needed to pack something more lethal than a couple of corroded road flares. But what did she know about weapons?

"I don't know. That was really weird. They boxed me in. But suddenly they were gone."

"I'll follow you home and make sure they don't bother you again. You have a cell phone, don't you?"

She nodded.

"Call your uncle Dave. He'll have some deputies at your house by the time we get there."

"You bet I will. I'm also gonna phone the National Guard and maybe even the Texas Rangers. Those guys scared me out of my socks."

Yes indeedy, she'd call the sheriff. Although without a tag number, and only a vague description of the vehicles, he wouldn't be able to do a stinkin' thing.

Chapter Twenty-One

"Are you absolutely positive you'll be okay?" Uncle Dave asked. "I still think I should call your mom. She could come out to stay with you."

"Don't do that." *Please don't!*

"How about Maizie?"

Even worse.

"I'll be fine, really I will. Stumpy's going to be right outside my gate. If I need anything, I'll holler." What was she going to do when the deputy went back to his regular duties? The sheriff's department couldn't guard her for the rest of her life.

"And, even though she's your wife and I know she'll give you holy hell if she finds out accidentally, please don't tell Aunt Eugenie." The last thing Liza needed was a deluge of family members. There wasn't much to be done about the rumor mill, but maybe she could hold off the circus until the morning.

"I think you're making a mistake, but if that's what you want, you got it," Dave said, shaking his head. "I'll call you tomorrow."

WATERY SUNSHINE STREAMED through the kitchen windows as Liza sipped her second cup of coffee. It had been the longest night of her life. Half a dozen times she'd picked up the phone to call Zack, and half a dozen times she'd slammed it down.

She had to be the most stubborn woman on the face of the

planet. It wasn't complicated. Make the call, and voilà, she'd have a hot guy with a gun—a great honkin' weapon—on the premises. But instead she'd prowled around checking locks, listening to her worthless dogs snore and acting like some kind of simpering coward. To be totally truthful, it came down to the fact Zack was more of a threat than the guys on the road. She didn't stand a chance against him.

Bang, bang, bang!

"Mother, are you up? Why is the door locked?" An early morning inquisition from Cassie was the perfect way to start the day. Note the sarcasm? "And why is the cop car out front?"

"Okay, give me a minute." Liza disarmed the security system and unlocked the door. She stepped aside to let the dogs scramble out and the kids race in.

The little rascals, Josh and Jason, had wormed their way into her heart to the point that she couldn't imagine life without them. Needless to say, she was thrilled they lived less than a quarter of a mile down the road.

"Who wants cinnamon rolls?" Her offer was met with a chorus of squeals.

Cassie followed the boys inside and headed straight to the coffeepot. "I'd rather have some answers. What's with Fort Knox?" She grabbed a mug from the cabinet. "Does it have anything to do with what I read in the paper this morning?" Cassie's voice was muffled as she reached into the refrigerator for the milk jug. "Did you know that a developer from outside Atlanta disappeared? The fruitcakes sent the paper some pictures, just like what's been happening here."

"No kidding?" Dealing with shotgun-toting pot growers was one thing. Having an up-close-and-personal encounter with a murderer would be an entirely different story. And God only knew where her current situation fit in.

"I don't think I have anything to worry about," Liza prevaricated with a completely straight face. She was surprised word of last night's debacle hadn't reached her daughter.

"Be careful, please," Cassie admonished. "You never know what the wackos will do next." She might be young, but Cassie was well on her way to becoming an über-mother.

"Why would anyone want to harm me?" Liza asked. And why would anyone want to run her off the road? Darn that little voice. "This isn't Atlanta. And besides, I have these wonderful watchdogs."

"Yeah, right. The vicious fur slugs are a lot of protection," Cassie said with a smile.

"They are." Liza's protest was halfhearted at best.

"Whatever. I'd better help the kids with the chores, or we'll never make it to our appointment. Come on, guys, let's get rolling." The boys each grabbed a pastry and made a mad dash to the barn.

Liza watched her beautiful daughter walk across the lawn. Rob had dearly loved his girls. He never would have left them. But that was a tale for another time. Fortunately, Cassie was distracted by the news report and had forgotten to pursue the subject of Liza's police protection.

One problem down. That left the situation with Zack. Why hadn't she mentioned him to Cassie? No hurry, she'd do that after she figured out what was happening. At this point she didn't know how to explain him even to herself. More than likely there wasn't anything *to* explain. He'd do his job and go back to California. Just as well, considering she was in a legal limbo that wasn't about to end.

No sooner had her daughter's minivan disappeared down the drive than the intercom connected to the outside gate squawked.

"Open up. The cavalry is here," Ruben demanded. Oh, dear, he rarely used his camp-commander voice.

Liza buzzed him in and peeked out the window. Almost in tandem, Ruben's Volvo and Zack's Expedition pulled up front. Zack was out of his SUV, striding to the porch before Ruben could manage to hop out of his car.

"Why didn't you call me?" he demanded, not bothering to hide his ire.

That was a valid question, and one she wasn't willing to answer. She needed a strong offense. Liza put her hands on her hips and assumed what Mama always called her stubborn face.

"Because I can take care of myself, that's why."

Zack grabbed her upper arms, then dropped his hands and stepped back. "That's garbage!"

"Children, children." Ruben had joined them on the veranda. "Liza, stop pitching a hissy, and, Maynard, you wait out here and count to a hundred. I'll fix us some iced tea and you can come on in when you've calmed down."

Liza and Ruben were already sitting at the table in the kitchen when Mr. Tall, Dark and Irritated stalked in and commandeered the nearest chair.

"Okay, let's think about this logically," Zack said. "Call it cop's intuition, or whatever, but I think the vandalism and last night's incident are two totally different situations." He shrugged before continuing. "Shooting at someone is an impersonal crime. Kidnapping is intimate, and the people last night got too close."

That was exactly what had kept Liza up all night. "So what do you suggest? I talked to Uncle Dave. He said his hands are tied. But I could tell he's worried, and frankly, I'm spooked."

"I think we have to bring in some professional security immediately. We've put off our Atlanta trip long enough. Do you still want to go with me?"

Darned straight she did. "Just tell me when, and I'll be ready."

"I'll make an appointment. I also want to chat with the people out at the Spirit of the Holy Protector. It won't hurt to put them on notice to stop harassing us."

"I'm going with you."

"No way!"

"Yes way!"

Ruben clanked a spoon against his glass. "You two are acting like a couple of Missouri jackasses. Zack, take Liza with you. They're not going to do anything in broad daylight."

Zack agreed, albeit somewhat reluctantly.

"And you," Ruben continued, pointing at Liza. "You need someone to stay out here with you at night."

"I'll do it," Zack volunteered.

"No!"

Ruben glared back and forth between the combatants. "Here's how it's gonna be. Zack will stay in your guest room until we figure out what's happening. And I don't want any more guff from either of you."

"Humph!" Fantastic. She'd been reduced to monosyllabic, nonsensical replies.

To be honest, she wasn't averse to having company. It was the thought that Zack might end up in her bed that scared her silly.

Chapter Twenty-Two

While Liza and crew were hashing out living arrangements, Harvey Spellman lurked outside the gate to Belle Meade. He was bored, tired, hungry and pissed. The schmucks on TV made stakeouts look glamorous. That was a crock. How in hell had he ended up in such a bind? The easy answer was that he'd wanted to keep his marijuana-growing operation a secret. But before he knew what had hit him, everything had spiraled out of control. Mama had told him not to make a deal with the devil, but was he smart enough to listen? Naw! Now he was up to his eyebrows in murder and kidnapping. And Magnolia Bluffs' version of Lucifer wasn't about to let him off easily. Blackmail sucked!

Then he got a lucky break. He realized that the gate wasn't latched—someone had been careless. He could sneak inside the fence, complete the assignment and head home for a hot meal. All he'd had to eat since last night was a Big Gulp and a Snickers bar, and his stomach was roaring like the MGM lion.

Harvey crept across the road and eased through a thicket of azaleas. He was supposed to check out Henderson's habits—where she went and what she did. Too bad they'd screwed up last time. The Volvo and the Expedition parked in the driveway meant she had company. But as long as he was careful, he'd be okay.

He crawled under the bushes next to the back porch. There were plenty of doors and windows, but they were probably all alarmed. Not that he couldn't work around that. Wasn't nothin' gonna stop old Harvey. Not when he had so much at stake.

LIZA WAS HALF LISTENING to Zack and Ruben when she noticed that P.B. was pacing back and forth, growling. Jelly was also in a frenzy.

"Hey, guys," she whispered, "look at the dogs. I think someone's outside."

Zack glanced at P.B. and quickly nodded. He whipped a gun out of his ankle holster.

Liza clutched her chest. "Dear Lord! You've been running around wearing that thing?"

"Lock yourself in the bathroom and call 911," he told her.

"Uh-uh. If you're going out there, so am I."

"I know what to do, and Ruben's going to help me. You'll just be in the way."

Ruben handed her the phone. "Call 911 and stay inside. Please."

At least he knew the magic word. That was more than she could say for the cretin who was ordering her around, even if he *was* right.

Zack gestured toward the French doors. "Are those locked?"

Liza shook her head.

"Ruben, I'm going to let P.B. out and I'll follow a second later. Hopefully his barking will run off the prowler. After I leave, you get the fireplace poker and head out the French doors," he instructed. "And, Liza, please, please don't come outside."

When he put it like that, she knew she'd stay put. What did she know about chasing bad guys, anyway?

HARVEY HUNKERED UNDER A LARGE shrub by the back door wondering if he should try the knob. Not that he was stupid enough to actually open it—not with all those people inside.

He might not get inside the gates again, so it was now or never.

It was the perfect time to find out if he could disable one of those fancy foreign cars. If her car broke down out on a deserted stretch of highway, they could snatch her without any witnesses.

He'd barely made it to the hood of the vehicle when the hounds of hell shot out of the house. At least that was how it sounded. Actually, it was one dog, barking loud enough to wake the dead. And right behind the big yellow canine was a gun-toting guy who didn't look in the mood for any crap.

Harvey might not be a rocket scientist, but he knew when to haul 'ass. He sprinted across the driveway, hurdling the fence on his way to the pasture. In his peripheral vision, he could see that a second dog had joined the chase and that both had wiggled under the barrier.

Damn, they were fast. Sure as shootin', he was dead meat. Then he noticed an outbuilding close to the edge of the forest. If he could get over the fence beyond the building, he might make it. The yellow dog was almost on his heels, but the little black one couldn't catch him.

Harvey vaulted the second fence, stumbled on the landing and ended up face-first in a huge pile of horse poop. He raised his head and glared at the dogs. They were sitting at the edge of the manure dump with their tongues lolling out. Harvey would've sworn the big one was grinning.

A piercing whistle got the canines' attention and they trotted back across the pasture. Two men came around the corner of the barn. It was time to leave.

ZACK BURST OUT LAUGHING. "I think the son of a gun landed in the shit this time."

Ruben hooted. In the distance, they heard a car peel out.

"Too bad the sheriff couldn't put out an APB on his smell," Zack said. "What else did you notice?"

"I didn't get a really good look, but he was tall, Caucasian and pudgy."

They were walking back to the house when the sheriff's deputy pulled into the drive.

"Hey, Weasel."

"Hey there, Ruben. Sheriff Dave radioed that he'll be here in about ten minutes. While we're waiting, why don't you give me a rundown on what happened?"

After Zack and Ruben gave him their version of the event, the deputy retraced the intruder's steps and found the place where the prowler had left his car. There was nothing left but a set of tire prints.

As a second police car roared up, a blue sedan quietly backed into an isolated copse of trees.

Chapter Twenty-Three

Life and business had to go on even though Zack's gut was screaming at him to haul Liza off to Timbuktu. As if that would really happen. So instead, the next morning he followed her back to the office. He and Ruben were scheduled for a chat with G. Harry.

Whoopee!

Zack had spent a frustrating night in Liza's guest room. He had a crick in his neck, a headache from lack of sleep and he probably looked like roadkill. He needed caffeine—badly. Some angel had made fresh pot of coffee and Zack was about to take his first sip when Ruben joined him in the kitchen.

"Are you ready for our trip to the county courthouse?"

"As ready as I'll ever be," Zack responded.

"I love your enthusiasm." Ruben didn't bother to suppress his chuckle.

"Shut it."

Ruben's chuckle changed into a full-blown laugh. "I like a guy who speaks his mind. Now, on another subject, Liza said you're going to Atlanta tomorrow to talk to the security firm."

"Yep, I want to interview the owner, and tomorrow's the first appointment she could offer."

"She?"

"Uh-huh, she," Zack said. "The company is supposed to be the best in the South. They'd better be. We need some help out here."

"We don't have the money for a big police force, but Dave Madison is doing the best he can with what he has. You know he'll protect Liza, even if he has to move in."

"I was impressed with him yesterday. I realize he has limited resources, and that's why I'm planning to stay at Belle Meade for as long as it takes. You and I both know he can't keep someone guarding her indefinitely."

"I can't tell you how much better that makes me feel. Our girl's a sitting duck out there with only those silly dogs to protect her." Ruben took a deep breath. "Okay, let's go tackle G. Harry."

"What are his specific interests?" Zack asked as he followed Ruben out to the car.

"Sex, sex and more sex."

"Unless he's a lot better-looking than I've heard, I don't expect he gets lucky very often."

"He's uglier than a bullfrog's butt. But that doesn't keep him from thinking he's a stud."

"Unbelievable," Zack muttered.

THE COURTHOUSE WAS A RED BRICK Victorian structure typical of government buildings in the South. Their footsteps echoed on the marble floors as they made their way through the crowded foyer. Zack must have made a disparaging sound because Ruben shot him a wry look.

"I know what you're thinking. The scum of the earth walks through here. Whenever I start wondering why I didn't go into criminal law, I come over here to watch the prisoners pass through. That answers all my what-ifs about career choice." He led Zack to the elevator. "The supervisors' offices are on the fourth floor."

Zack was accustomed to the vagaries of big-city life, but some of the things he had encountered in Magnolia Bluffs bordered on the surreal. And that proved especially true in the case of the tall, cadaverous man who met them at the door. He was a human version of a vulture.

"Hello, there. G. Harry Middleton," he boomed, stepping into the hall. The offer of a handshake was noticeably absent. "Beth, rustle up some refreshments," he yelled at his harried assistant before waving his visitors into his office.

"Sit, sit." He motioned to two straight-backed wooden chairs in front of a large mahogany desk. Zack had run into guys like him before. They got off on intimidation—subtle and not so subtle.

Ruben winked at Beth when she reappeared with a pot of coffee and three dainty china cups and saucers.

"Put it on the credenza, and make sure I'm not disturbed for at least fifteen minutes," G. Harry ordered, then turned his attention to his guests. "Do you take your coffee black or all doctored up?" He sauntered to the credenza to dispense the libations. "Personally, I think it's a crime to ruin good coffee with milk."

Did anyone really care what the fool thought? Although G. Harry was a huge pain in the rear, Zack figured it wouldn't be too smart to antagonize him, unless he laid so much as a pinkie on Liza. Then all bets were off.

"Black or with milk and sugar?" he asked again. Patience apparently wasn't his strong suit.

"Lots of milk and three spoons of sugar, please," Zack replied, even though he preferred his coffee black.

"Ruben?"

"Oh, black, definitely black." Ruben was obviously struggling to keep a straight face.

"Thank you for taking time out of your busy day to see us." Ruben fell into the obsequious demeanor the politician clearly expected.

"I don't have long for this, so you can skip the details. I had the staff brief me. I'll tell you right up front, I'm going to be a hard man to convince." He shot his cuffs to punctuate his announcement.

Who did he think he was—Prince Charles?

"I don't think we need any more people in this county. And

we particularly don't want city people to move out here and commute to work."

He leaned back, clasping his hands behind his head. "Pull out those maps and let's talk about the 'voluntary' contributions you're planning to make if your project gets the go-ahead."

Ruben had just started the presentation when G. Harry interrupted. "I've seen enough. I'm already late for another meeting." He rose. "Ruben, where is that good-looking partner of yours?" Without waiting for an answer, he marched out the door.

Zack made an exaggerated show of wiping the sweat off his brow. "After all that fun, I need a beer. Let's run by the office and pick up Liza."

LIZA HEARD THE CAR AND WAS waiting at the front door when Ruben walked in. "How did things go?" She watched Zack as he rummaged in the back of his SUV.

"G. Harry asked about you. He wondered if you'd be interested in a roll in the hay."

"Oh, really? How nice," she murmured, leaning out the door for a better look at Zack's tush. And what a tush it was!

Ruben leaned against the cabinet. "He also told me to tell you he's got a room over at the Pine Tree. The two of you can go there and have a little tête-à-tête."

"Hmm."

Ruben's laughter finally caught her attention. "What's so funny?"

"You. I just told you G. Harry wants you to get acquainted with his John Thomas and you didn't bat an eyelash. Must be something awfully interesting out in the parking lot." Ruben's belly laughs kept rolling while Liza glared at him, hands on her hips.

"What's so funny?" Zack asked.

Ruben couldn't speak—all that came out was another guffaw.

"Not a thing," Liza snapped, spinning to face Zack. "He's being a wise-ass."

Ruben responded with another bout of laughter.

"And not a word out of you or you're a dead man," she threatened.

Ruben wisely made an exit.

Zack followed Liza into her office. "Ruben and I were talking about going to the pub for a beer and dinner." He strolled around the desk to nuzzle her neck. "How about it, are you up for a drink?" he asked, running his fingers through her hair.

It was bad enough that he was camping out in her guest room, now he was caressing her. She closed her eyes, anticipating a kiss.

"You guys ready to go, or what?" Ruben reappeared like a bad rash. Darn his hide! He normally had the timing of a rattlesnake. When he made a strange chuckling noise, Liza was ready to do him bodily harm.

"I believe he's telling us something. What do you think?" Zack plunked a soft kiss on her forehead before towing her out the door. "Let's go before we get in trouble."

ALTHOUGH GILLY'S PUB WAS crowded, they were able to find a table. "Is beer okay with you guys?" At Zack and Liza's thumbs-up, Ruben summoned a harried waitress and placed their order.

"Tell me everything that happened." Liza shot Ruben a glare. "Not you."

"I have to say it was an experience." Zack paused until the waitress placed a pitcher of cold beer and three frosty mugs on the table. "I'm not sure how the man got elected. And I wouldn't be surprised at anything he might pull." Zack pushed his mug toward Ruben. "Fill it up."

Liza waited until Zack's mug was full before she asked the key question. "Do you think he could be involved in what's happening?"

Zack hesitated a little too long before answering. "You can't discount anyone. But let me put your mind at ease. As long as we can keep this project viable, the Norton Company won't bail. We can handle the vandalism. The supervisors, on the other hand, could very well ax the entire thing. And most of all, I'm worried about you."

Liza's response was cut short when a man walked up, strutting as if he owned the world. Perhaps he did. He wore a designer sweater that screamed money.

"Ruben, Miss Henderson." After the perfunctory niceties, the man turned to Liza. "I've left you several messages, but you haven't returned my calls. I'd like you to help me with a business deal I have going on out in Dalton County."

"I've been busy. Charlie's out of town, and I'm working almost full-time on another project. I'm afraid we can't take on any other clients. Perhaps you can find someone in Atlanta."

"You couldn't make an exception, just this once?"

"Nope, I'm really overwhelmed. Sorry." Liza turned her head in obvious dismissal.

Zack wondered when her Southern manners had taken a hike. The guy was obviously a wealthy developer, and Liza had more than likely known him all her life.

The man nodded once before walking away.

Zack's curiosity was killing him. "I've never seen you be rude to anyone before."

"I'll do it again. He might look like a legitimate businessman, but he's slimy. If he can cut a corner or pull one over on the folks in charge, he'll do it. Charlie and I have decided to blackball him."

"He obviously doesn't realize that."

"Nope, it's on a need-to-know basis," Liza admitted. "Let's discuss something else. He makes me irritable."

"We don't want her to get crabby," Ruben put in.

"Can it!" Liza scowled, but ruined the effect by giggling.

THE SUN WAS SETTING WHEN THEY left the tavern. Ruben suddenly pointed at a nondescript blue sedan that was idling at the curb.

"See that car? It's been on our street every day this week." Before

Zack could stop him, Ruben stalked toward the car. He hadn't made it two steps before the vehicle shot out of the parking space.

"Did you see that?" Ruben was standing in the middle of the street, while Liza and Zack stared at the retreating taillights. "He didn't want to talk to us."

"Do you think that's related to what happened last night?" Liza asked.

Zack didn't know, but he certainly intended to find out.

Chapter Twenty-Four

Early the next morning, Zack and Liza braved the Atlanta rush hour to drive to the security firm's office. Procrastination was no longer an option. The office was located in a high-rise in the trendy Buckhead area. Zack took one look at the decorator's dream of chrome and glass and saw dollar signs.

He checked in with the receptionist before joining Liza on a sofa shaped like a high-heeled shoe.

"This is the most uncomfortable-looking couch I've ever seen," Zack said. He did a trial bounce and discovered it was as hard as a brick.

Although private security firms were outside his area of expertise, this wasn't at all what he'd expected. Even the blond receptionist could've passed for a Miss Georgia contestant. The only thing missing was her sash reading Miss Macon.

"Mr. Maynard, Mrs. Henderson. Would you please follow me to Miss DuBois' office?" The beauty queen led them past a fortune in contemporary art. Zack wasn't exactly a country bumpkin, but modern art was definitely not in his comfort zone. He silently noted a piece featuring a doghouse and various dismembered body parts.

"Don't you dare laugh, you hear me?" Liza whispered, although she was obviously struggling to hold in her own giggles.

"This is Miss DuBois' office." The receptionist ushered them in before disappearing down the hall in a cloud of Obsession. Zack recognized the perfume because Angela bought it by the gallons.

A Grace Kelly look-alike sat behind a massive desk. Where were the guys, the guns and the smoke-filled cubicles? This place looked more like the corporate offices of Mary Kay than a top-shelf private security firm.

Zack's thought must have shown on his face because the blonde smiled as she came around the desk. "Don't look so distressed." She shook hands with Zack and Liza. "We're very good at what we do. That's why we're so expensive. And don't worry. Our people have guns and concealed-weapons permits. Most of them used to work at Atlanta PD."

That made him feel better.

An hour and a half later, they climbed back into the car, satisfied they were about to get some much-needed assistance.

"We're doing the right thing," Zack said, maneuvering his way through traffic to the freeway. At least he hoped so for Liza's sake. She needed to get her life back to normal.

"Do you think they can really help us?"

"For what they're charging, they'd better."

"And that's another thing. I want to pay for it."

"Nope. This is on my tab. I have plenty of money. And since I'm a part owner in Norton Development, it's my responsibility to make sure things go smoothly."

Liza wasn't quite sure she agreed, but it was his call. And did it really matter? As soon as their business was finished, he'd leave Magnolia Bluffs. And yet another person she cared about would be walking away from her. But he'd never made any kind of commitment, so how could he technically desert her?

"What do you think we'll find when we talk to Brother Turnipseed?" That was the other question she'd been dying to ask.

"I'm not sure. I do think we should let someone know where we're going."

Liza's thought exactly. She assumed the members of the religious group were harmless, but...

THAT WAS THE END OF MEANINGFUL conversation until they got back to Belle Meade. The sun was dipping beneath the horizon as they sat on the dock, skipping rocks across the water.

"I needed to get away from here even if it was to interview a security specialist," Liza admitted.

Zack was still bunking in her guest room—darn it! What did she have to do to get him into her bed? Whoa! Slow down there!

And had he really stocked up on protection as he'd said he would? Another big whoa! The man had more baggage than a Samsonite shop. It was lucky they hadn't progressed past that first steamy kiss. Who was she kidding? She was frustrated! Even though there wasn't any future for them, she could feel her resolve weakening.

Zack threw a stick into the water for P.B. to fetch.

"You know what happens next, don't you?" Liza scooted back as the dog dropped his prize at Zack's feet. P.B. shook his entire body, flinging tiny drops of water in every direction.

Jelly stared disdainfully at her wet friend.

"He'll have you doing that for hours if you let him."

Zack tossed the stick again. P.B. retrieved the twig and dropped it on the deck. Then he plopped on his haunches, quivering in anticipation.

"I told you so." Liza scratched the dog's wet ears. "The only way to stop this game is for us to go back to the house."

Zack thought for a second. House, bed, couch, bed, horizontal surface. "Why don't we stay down here a bit longer?" He was trying to do the right thing.

Her delectable lips were begging to be kissed. *Nope.* As much as he wanted to, she'd have to make the first move.

"Let's talk about your family."

"My family?" she asked.

"Yeah." He leaned back, like a man who had all day.

"Okay, if that's what you want. I've told you about Rob and the girls. And you've met Mama and Maizie. What else can I say?"

Liza's expression said she knew Zack was looking for a distraction. "Tell me more about your children." He was fairly sure that was a request she couldn't resist.

"My girls have their dad's overpowering personality. They can be a handful, but all in all, they're wonderful young women." Liza put Jelly in her lap. "I'm sure you know all about family dynamics. Somehow, I got stuck in the role of the sensible member. I planned the trips and paid the bills." She rubbed the dog's ears. "And believe it or not, that's not the real me."

"Is that right?"

There was a pensive silence before she continued. "Here's something I've never told anyone, and just thinking it makes me feel guilty. At times I felt invisible, as though my true self was fading out of the picture." She brushed her hands together. "Enough big confessions. Now it's your turn. I want to hear about your ex-wife."

Turnabout was fair play. He supposed he could pony up.

"Her name is Angela." Zack shrugged. "It was a mistake from the beginning. We had different values, different tastes and different goals. In fact, we were total opposites. And her family didn't help matters." He flashed her a wry smile.

"I won't say anything bad about her, but I don't mind criticizing her parents. Her father's family was in California before the Gold Rush and her mother is a shameless social climber. Although they want everyone to think they're blue bloods, the truth is they're flat broke. That's not a great combo."

He was interrupted by another shower of water, courtesy of P.B. "I took Angela to Kansas a couple of times. She griped the whole time we were there. She hated everything—the heat, the people, the wheat fields and most of all, the pickup trucks." He grinned at the memory and his dimples appeared. "One time we got stuck in a storm and were pummeled by hailstones the size of golf balls. That really got her complaining. After our marriage started falling apart, I was sorry she'd missed the blizzards and the tornadoes."

"Did your family like her?"

"The day I called Mom and told her about the divorce, she snorted. But it was an eloquent snort."

"Is she beautiful?" Liza asked quietly, as though not sure she wanted to hear the answer.

"She's astonishingly beautiful, if you only look on the surface. Somewhere along the way I think she lost part of her soul. She's missing the intangible quality that makes people truly beautiful, like you are."

HE THOUGHT SHE WAS BEAUTIFUL. As much as Liza hated to admit it—even to herself—the feeling was mutual.

Zack took her hand. "In case you were wondering, I've never thought of you as the sensible one."

Liza wasn't quite sure that was a compliment. "Thank you. I think."

He had the temerity to laugh. "I presume your family doesn't realize I've moved out here, at least temporarily."

"I think Daddy might know, but Mama doesn't have a clue. If she did, she'd have us picking out a new silver pattern, and I already have enough silver to serve half the county."

He was close enough to run his hand up her arm, continuing his journey along the lapels of her polo. "Would we have to pick out a silver pattern if we did this?" He trailed a finger down the placket of her shirt, drawing her closer.

The things that man could do with his lips made her mouth go dry and had her stomach doing funny little back flips. And when Liza imagined them naked, hot and sweaty, doing the wild thing, she almost had a heart attack.

She and Rob had never bothered to discuss their sex life. It had just seemed to happen. Even at the ripe old age of forty-four, Liza wasn't sure she was mature enough for mental foreplay.

"Why don't we have a glass of wine?" She pulled back in order to get some breathing room. Wine would be good. It would give her a chance to think. Did she or didn't she want to do this? Should she or shouldn't she? Maybe she should just go straight for a lobotomy. That would put them both out of their misery. Although Zack didn't seem miserable. On the contrary, he looked like a very sexy tomcat with a thick bowl of cream.

Zack held his hands up in surrender and followed her to the house.

"White or red?" She took two bottles from the rack in the kitchen and held them up for his inspection. He peered at one bottle, then the next, and took them both, placing them on the countertop. Before she could react he had her in his arms.

"I'm really more hungry than thirsty."

She couldn't resist his sinful eyes with their little flecks of blue and green. Whether this was what she should do, or not, it was inevitable. She'd follow her heart and worry about the consequences later.

Despite the endless internal arguments she'd waged, and the list of reasons she shouldn't get involved, Liza knew she was a goner. The man took kissing to a whole new dimension. And those talented, talented hands. Oh, my, those big, calloused, talented, sexy hands.

"The couch," Liza muttered as she backed toward the overstuffed sofa and fell onto the cushions, taking him down with her.

Zack deftly flipped her so she was on top. But when he reached for the hem of her shirt, she froze. What if he didn't like what he saw?

"You're thinking too much," he mumbled. "Don't cover yourself. You're beautiful and I want to see you." He nuzzled between her breasts and slowly kissed his way from one to the other.

That was easy enough for him to say. Guys didn't have to

worry about saggy boobs and cellulite. It'd been a long time since a man had seen her naked, and she wasn't twenty years old anymore. She'd nursed two children and gravity had definitely taken its toll.

As he worked from one erotic spot to another, he managed to dispel her trepidation. The man was obviously delighted with her. Liza relaxed and fumbled with his button and zipper. There were some things a girl never forgot, no matter how long it had been.

"This time I'm prepared." He reached into his pocket and retrieved several foil packets just as Liza pushed his jeans down.

"Hmm. That's nice. Now hurry up and get out of that shirt." She ran a hand up his oh-so-scrumptious hairy chest. "There's nothing like a butt-naked Boy Scout."

ZACK ROLLED OFF AND PULLED Liza close, back to front. Now this was nirvana. He'd close his eyes long enough to recuperate, and then he'd tell her how incredible she was, he thought as he drifted off to sleep.

His fuzzy brain registered the fact someone was licking his neck in long wet strokes. There was something incredibly cold resting above his collarbone.

"God, baby, I couldn't get it up if you threatened me with a gun." He cracked an eye and stared into a pair of chocolate-brown eyes, accompanied by a wet nose and a mountain of yellow fur.

Liza peered over Zack's chest as P.B. gave her his best doggy grin.

"A gun, huh?" A wave of mirth overtook her. She held her stomach, trying to stop laughing, but every time she breathed, peals of giggles erupted until tears ran down her cheek.

"Okay, little darlin', you're coming with me." He stood and pulled her up with him.

"And where might we be going?" she asked, even though she had a sneaking suspicion she knew the answer. And, if she was right, it would be delightful.

"Upstairs, where I'm sure there's a great place to take a shower together. And then later, if you can find your Glock, maybe you can convince me to entertain you."

Chapter Twenty-Five

"Race you to the barn. The loser has to muck the stalls," Josh yelled to his brother. His bicycle skimmed across the gravel. Riding their bikes to the barn was a Saturday-morning ritual that the kids looked forward to all week. There was always the chance they could talk Grammy into taking them into town for doughnuts. And what kid didn't love a gooey doughnut?

"No fair! You have a head start!" Jason was pumping his legs as hard as he could. Being beaten by his brother at anything wasn't acceptable. Neck and neck, they rounded the bend in the driveway and slid to a tie at the barn gate.

"I won!" Josh crowed. "Let's go find Grammy." He didn't bother to wait for his brother. Not to be outdone, Jason ran as fast as he could. Even though it was early, P.B. and Jelly were already on greeter duty.

In typical kid fashion, Josh and Jason did a little pushing and shoving as they walked up to the back door. That is, until Josh glanced through the glass pane and came to an abrupt halt.

He grabbed his brother's shirt collar and pulled them both under the rhododendron beside the door.

"Keep your head down and be real quiet, but peek in and tell me what you see," he whispered.

Jason didn't know what he was supposed to be looking for, but his brother had on his serious voice. He inched up to the door until he could see in the window. What he saw scared the snot out of him. He ducked and crawled back under the bush.

"There's a huge guy in there, and he's got a knife. Do you think he's kidnapped Grammy?" The blood drained from his face. "What should we do?"

P.B. flopped to his belly and scooted under the bush, giving both boys wet puppy kisses.

Wiping their faces on their sleeves, in unison they grumbled at him to get away. But P.B. put his head on his paws, waiting for the fun to start.

Josh put his arms around the big dog's neck for comfort.

"Let's think about this," Jason whispered. "There aren't any strange cars, so we know he's not visiting."

"Yeah," Josh agreed.

"We saw a guy in our grandma's kitchen with a knife, right?"

Although Josh hadn't actually seen the knife, he believed his brother. "Right."

"And we didn't see our grandma."

"Uh-huh."

"Why don't we look again, just to make sure she's not in there? You stick your head up. You're closest."

"Why me? You're the oldest," Josh argued.

"But you're the closest."

"Oh, fudge," Josh grumbled. "Okay, here goes." He shimmied out from under the bush. P.B. was close on his heels. Sneaking to the door, he popped his head up, scanned the room and immediately dropped to the porch when P.B. started barking. He grabbed Jason's shirttail and ran toward the end of the house.

"He's coming out. He heard P.B. and he's coming out with his knife." Josh was in danger of peeing in his pants. Oh, sugar! Kids his age *didn't* pee their pants. He took one look at his brother's face and saw his own panic reflected there.

The back door opened and P.B. raced inside. Stupid dog! Give him a bowl of kibbles and he'd be your friend for life.

The boys ran to their bicycles, mindful to keep out of sight.

"Do you think he killed her?" Josh whispered.

"I don't know. Maybe he's holding her for ransom. We've got to tell Mom and Dad."

The boys made it home in record time. They jumped on the queen-size bed where Cassie was trying to sleep.

"What are you guys doing?" She wanted to pull the covers over her head, but she realized it was a losing battle. No more sweet dreams, just a couple of kids who smelled like dead fish.

They pummeled her with information. "There's a crazy man in Grammy's house!"

"He kidnapped her and he's got a knife about this big." Josh held his hands two feet apart. "We've got to call the cops, 'cause he's gonna get away."

Cassie jackknifed up, putting her hands on her head. "Wait! What do you mean, there's a man in Mother's house? Where was he, and what was he doing?" Even though the boys sometimes exaggerated, Cassie was about to hit the panic button. "Start from the beginning, slow down and tell me everything."

Both boys were jabbering.

"Hold it!" she yelled. "One at a time. Jason, you start." He was the most analytical of the duo.

"We went to feed the ponies, and then Josh decided he wanted doughnuts so he tried to beat me to the back door, and then we saw this guy in the kitchen, and he was waving a big knife around."

Josh piped up. "So we jumped in the bushes, but P.B. tried to get in with us and then this guy came to the back door with his knife and we thought we were going to get caught, so we ran as quick as we could to tell you to call the cops."

"We want to save Grammy," Jason said with a sob.

Cassie's heart was beating about a thousand miles an hour. She had to make sure this wasn't one of the kids' tall tales. With a calm that hid her increasing panic, Cassie quietly asked, "At any time did you see your grandmother?"

"No!" they shouted in unison.

"Did you see any strange cars in the driveway, anything like a repair truck? Maybe the guy was working on the dishwasher or something."

Josh became impatient with the questioning and grabbed Cassie's hand to drag her to the phone. "There wasn't any car, and he wasn't a repairman. Please, please, Mom, call the cops."

That did it! Cassie grabbed a pair of jeans and scrambled around looking for a pair of shoes. She finally located a tennis shoe under the bed and a hiking boot in the closet. Not the best, but it would have to do.

"One of you guys call your dad at his office and tell him exactly what you told me. Let him know I'm on my way over to Mother's, and that he needs to meet me there. Tell him to call Uncle Dave. Can you do all that? And most important, I want you both to stay right here. Do you understand? Right here in this house. Absolutely do not leave the house!"

Cassie grabbed Jim's baseball bat as she ran out the front door. She decided she could get to her mother's place faster by riding her bike across the shortcut.

After hiding the bicycle behind the barn, Cassie crept furtively to the back terrace. From there she crawled across the brick patio to peek in the living room windows. She had to be very, very quiet.

The kids were right. Even the dogs weren't out. Oh God, she prayed the maniac hadn't killed everyone. The only vehicle in the driveway was Liza's old pickup.

First things first. She had to find out if only one person was involved. That would make a big difference in how the police responded. Cassie crawled under the azaleas toward the glass-enclosed breakfast room. When she popped up, she caught a glimpse of a man heading toward the back door.

He was trying to get away! Cassie peered around the end of the house and watched him saunter out to the driveway. He had a set of keys in his hand, and he was half-naked. Lord in heaven—no shirt, no shoes, and he strolled out of her mom's house as if he owned the place. Cassie took a deep breath. This was no time to faint. He could be a serial killer!

The man walked over to the pickup and fumbled with the lock. More than likely, he was trying to add car theft to his list of crimes. With her heart in her throat, Cassie tiptoed across the lawn and jabbed the small end of the baseball bat into his back.

"Get your hands in the air. Don't move and don't turn around. That would make me nervous, and this gun might go off if I get jittery." Jeez, she sounded like a bad Chuck Norris movie. Hallelujah! It worked. The man slowly raised his hands and faced the pickup, keeping completely still.

WHAT WAS HAPPENING NOW? Zack was fairly sure whatever was poking him in the back wasn't a gun. But he also didn't think it was worth taking a chance. If the dingbat really had a gun, and she managed to pull the trigger, a Mack truck could drive through what would be left of him.

Zack stared at the pickup. Maybe she wanted Oscar. He couldn't imagine why anyone would steal that piece of junk, but different strokes and all that B.S.

He jingled the keys. "Here are the keys if that's what you're after. You can take the truck and leave."

"I don't want the pickup, you dummy. I want you to be quiet until the sheriff gets here."

A siren wailed in the distance. Zack put his hands on top of his head. Bedlam seemed to be an everyday occurrence in Liza's world.

Liza ran out the back door with the dogs bouncing around her feet. "Cassandra McGuire, what *are* you doing with that baseball bat? Drop it right now!"

Cassie wheeled around, digging the bat harder into Zack's back.

"Ohmigod! Mom, are you all right? If he's hurt you, I'll kill him right now. I can whack him upside the head. No jury in the world would convict me."

The police car screeched in and a freckle-faced sheriff's deputy jumped out and ran toward the action, gun drawn.

"Step aside, ma'am, I've got him covered." Both women went still, staring at the rookie.

Without moving a muscle, Zack demanded, "Before anyone decides to throw me in the slammer, do you think I could get a shirt and find out what the hell is happening?" His voice got louder and more emphatic with each word. "Liza, would you please explain to them who I am?"

Cassie looked from her mother, who was dressed only in an oversize man's shirt, to the man who was clad in a pair of Dockers. Her mouth fell open. "Oh, no!" She dropped the baseball bat and covered her eyes with her hands.

The deputy lowered his gun. "What's happenin'?"

Before anyone could answer him, Cassie's husband's car pulled in, barely missing the police cruiser. He ran to Cassie and folded her in his arms.

"Oh, Jimmy, I'm so embarrassed."

Jim looked from Liza, to Zack, to Cassie and then back to the deputy.

He obviously figured out what was going on. "There's nothing to worry about. We can take care of this."

"Are you positive, Dr. Jim?"

"Yes, everything's fine. There's been a misunderstanding. Why don't you call the sheriff and tell him not to bother coming out. I'm sure he's on his way, right?" he asked, trying to disentangle himself from his wife.

"Yes, sir. I'll radio him right now."

Cassie burrowed her head in her husband's shirt and whispered, "I think my mom had sex." She sniffled again. "My mother!"

"Cassandra!" Liza said, barely refraining from rolling her eyes.

Jim lifted his wife's chin. "Perhaps we should have a little talk about age. She's only nine years older than I am."

They were saved from further discussion when the deputy

strolled back. "Sheriff Dave asked me to tell you that he'll call you later. He said that if you don't watch out, you're gonna be on our frequent call list. Y'all take care now, ya hear." The deputy hopped into his cruiser and sped out of the drive.

Chapter Twenty-Six

Like most family brouhahas, the excitement eventually subsided. After Liza sent Cassie and her crew on their way, the rest of the day passed without any additional commotion.

"There's never a dull moment around here," Zack said as they snuggled on a chaise longue watching the sunset.

"No, there isn't. This morning was humiliating." Liza closed her eyes and stroked his cheeks. The bristly stubble was fascinating. "My girls can be a bit melodramatic. Just wait till you meet Kara," she said with a laugh. "Cassie's bad enough, but Kara's our real drama queen." She wiggled closer to his groin.

"If you don't stop that, we won't be out here long." Zack adjusted his position, and then rubbed her ring finger. "When did you stop wearing your wedding band?"

Liza studied her hand. "About two years ago. It was my mother-in-law's idea. A year after Rob disappeared, she took me to dinner without the girls. She made sure we were in a public place before she started in on me and told me it was time to get back to the land of the living. She also informed me that I needed to take off the ring and start dating. I know it broke her heart to say it, but she's a pragmatist." Liza turned to face him.

"She sold me this place. Actually, it was more like a present. We were in a really tight financial situation. I couldn't collect on

Rob's life insurance or his Social Security or anything. It was touch-and-go for a while."

"That had to be tough."

"Yeah."

"So she expects you to date. That's liberal minded, don't you think?" Zack asked.

"Mimi's an extraordinary woman."

Liza started to rub Zack's chest, but he took her hands. He wanted to hear this story, and if she kept that up, conversation would come to a halt.

"What would she think about you getting married?" The question popped out without the benefit of having his brain in gear. He couldn't contemplate anything serious, at least not until he got Angela off his back. And as for marriage, he'd have to do some soul-searching before he entertained that idea.

She cuddled closer. "Married? Oh, I imagine she'd be thrilled, just as long as I didn't move too far away. That's all a moot point, anyway. Legally, I can't do anything for at least a year." Liza sat up. "You know, I think she was one of the few people who really understood Rob. He always rushed headlong into life, grabbing everything he could with a gusto that left me breathless. In a way, it scares me that the girls are so much like him. But enough of that. Let's go for dinner."

Liza had had enough introspection for one evening. Soon— very soon—she'd get her head on straight, and then she'd decide what to do about whatever it was they had going on. Intellectually she realized there was no future for them. What man in his right mind would want to get mixed up in all her issues?

"I'd kill for a big old slab of ribs. Cracker Jack's has the best barbecue around, if you don't mind eating with your fingers." She was rambling again, but sometimes a girl had to go for the non-sensical. "I'll change into some jeans."

Zack nuzzled her neck. "If you're planning to get rid of your clothes, why don't we take advantage of the opportunity?"

"What about dinner?" She moved her head to offer him better access.

"A very late dinner sounds good." He kissed his way down her collarbone.

"Uh-huh." Rational comment was beyond her. She vaguely registered the fact he was unbuttoning her blouse and kissing his way around the edges of her bra.

"Wait a minute, I have an idea." She was surprised she could remember her own name, but with what little bit of sanity she had left, she marched into the kitchen and grabbed a chilled bottle of wine and a pan of brownies. Then she found a corkscrew and two crystal flutes.

"What are you waiting for? Let's go upstairs. I have two of the major food groups right here." She gave him her very best bad-girl wink. "I'm sure you can get creative." She scampered toward the stairs. Of course, Zack was right behind her.

LIZA LEANED ON HER ELBOW, watching Zack nap. Jelly was tucked up around his long legs. This was getting out of hand. Every time she saw him, her adrenaline surged and her heart beat madly. Her brain got fuzzy with each touch, and when he smiled, she melted like a Dairy Queen dip-top cone.

She flopped back on the pillow, flinging her arm over her eyes. This could turn out to be a terrible disaster. She was falling in love with an intensity that scared her silly. What was going to happen when he went back to San Francisco? He obviously cared about her. He couldn't do the things he did and not harbor some kind of feeling. But he hadn't said he loved her. And more important, he hadn't said he was staying.

She must have made a noise because he rolled over and threaded his fingers through her hair.

"Hey, little elf, let's go get those ribs. I seem to have worked up an appetite." He pulled her down for a kiss. "Then we can come back here for some dessert."

"I THOUGHT I'D FIND YOU HERE. The grapevine is a little slow on weekends. It took over a day for word to filter to Atlanta."

Zack lowered his coffee cup and gaped at the girl standing in the doorway. The Viking goddess was at least six feet tall with waist-length platinum-blond hair. She was wearing a gauzy purple-and-gold belly-dancing outfit that covered the most important anatomical parts, but left a broad expanse of golden skin open to view.

"You must be Zack. Cassie called me. I'm Kara." She floated forward on bare feet. "I'm Cassie's sister. Anyway, I decided I'd better come down and find out what your intentions are. Cass sucks at this. She thinks the best of everyone. Not like me."

Zack snapped his jaw shut.

"I'm Zack. Your mom went into town while I was in the shower. She said something about a chocolate doughnut and dying. She should be back in a few minutes."

Kara propped her hands on her hips. "Just what, may I ask, were you doing in my mother's shower? She's not very sophisticated about—" she did an eloquent hand wave "—you know, this sort of thing. Cassie and I feel like we have a responsibility to take care of her."

"Really." Zack took a big gulp of coffee, wondering how to handle this one. His first urge was to laugh, but thankfully, he controlled himself. The kid obviously thought she was the family guardian angel, ready to protect the weak and the addlepated, which apparently included Liza. And what a guardian angel; even Lucifer would drool. He wondered if she had her mother's sense of humor, and whether it would be prudent to tease her. It probably wasn't smart, but the impulse got the best of him.

"In answer to the first question, a shower always feels good after a night of hot, wild sex. As for your second statement, yes, she is sophisticated about this sort of thing. And believe me, she's definitely able to take care of herself."

It was little Miss Harem's turn to gape. "But parents aren't supposed to, uh…and if they do, they don't talk about it, and it sure isn't hot and…" she sputtered. "Especially not my *mother!* You might not realize it, but she's over forty!"

Zack patted the chair next to him. "You sound like Cassie. Why don't we sit down and get acquainted. And let me tell you about life after thirty-five."

LIZA GLANCED AT THE TWO WHITE bakery sacks on the front seat. After last night, she had to have chocolate and sugar and gooey, creamy, fattening stuff. If this madness continued she'd weigh three hundred pounds. But what a glorious three hundred pounds it would be.

Crap-a-diddle! Kara was home. Liza knew she should have called her youngest daughter before the gossip reached her. But it was too late for that, so she'd have to fake it. Confidence could cover a lot of embarrassing situations. How long had they been talking? Slowly, very slowly, she trudged inside.

"How's my baby?" Liza rose on tiptoe to kiss her daughter on the cheek. "I see you guys have met. I brought doughnuts, éclairs and apple fritters. That's a great outfit, Kara. When did you get here?"

Zack put his arm around Liza's waist. "You're nattering. Kara was telling me about school. She's on her way to a street fair."

Liza fumbled through the wrong drawer for the forks. "Is that why you're wearing your belly-dancing outfit?"

"Uh-huh. My roomie and I are doing a demonstration. But I thought I should come down to check on you. Now that I see you're okay, I've got to run. Our show's on at one, and I have to go by my apartment first. I'm really pleased to meet you." Kara extended her hand to Zack. "I imagine I'll see you here again, soon." She gave Liza a hug. "Love you, Mom. Behave, now, ya hear." With that, she raced to her car.

Chapter Twenty-Seven

Liza now knew what it would be like to be a hamster on a wheel. On almost every level, her life was running willy-nilly. It wasn't boring; it wasn't staid. It also wasn't completely under her control.

Whew!

As much as Liza hated to do it, Monday morning she and Zack were on their way to Blackwater Lake to check out the neighbors one more time. The closer they got to the Spirit of the Holy Protector church, the more nervous she became. She wasn't absolutely positive Brother Turnipseed had a pit of timber rattlers, but just the thought of the squirmy creatures gave her chills. Big snakes, small snakes, harmless snakes, poisonous snakes—even worms made her jittery. Liza flat-out hated reptiles.

"Do you really think is a good idea?" she asked.

Zack glanced her way. "You're white as a ghost. Do you want to go home?"

"No. We need to ask them point-blank if they know what's happening." In theory it sounded perfect. As long as *snakes* weren't involved!

The ramshackle single-wide trailer didn't look any better in the daylight than it had at night. The hard-baked, grassless yard still sported a blocked-up Ford Escort and a derelict washing machine. The three coonhounds asleep on the wooden steps and the cat basking on the top of an old tire were a new addition. She hadn't seen them the night she and her cohorts had tried their hands at undercover work.

Liza parked behind a pickup that was even more rusted than her own. The dogs broke into a chorus of howls.

Zack studied the hounds. "Do you think they bite?"

"Beats me." She was relieved they didn't slither.

"Okay, here goes." He opened the pickup door and stepped out. "Dogs have always liked me. Hope my luck holds."

He was saved from testing his luck when Brother Turnipseed moseyed out onto the porch.

Although Liza had never actually seen the preacher, she'd heard a lot about him. She still wasn't prepared for the reality. The man was huge, hairy and wearing nothing but a pair of dirty overalls. He was sans shirt, shoes and teeth.

"Good grief," she mumbled, but Zack apparently heard her.

"You want to stay in the truck?"

"No way. I wouldn't miss this for the world."

When their master whistled, the dogs wandered under the wooden porch.

"Howdy, folks. I know who you are, little lady, but I don't rightly know your friend." He stuck out a beefy paw. "I'm Calvin Turnipseed, but my flock calls me Brother. That there's my church." He nodded toward a building on the other side of the gravel lane.

"Why don't ya come over out of the sun and sit a spell." He indicated a couple of beat-up metal lawn chairs under an ancient live oak.

They followed their host to the shade.

"Have a seat and I'll go fetch us some cold Cokes."

"Great, I'd love that." The reprieve gave her an opportunity to let Zack know she could interpret, if necessary. But before Liza could ask if he understood Redneck, Calvin returned clutching three bottles of soda.

"Here ya go." The preacher gave them the soft drinks,

chugged half his own bottle and leaned back with a satisfied belch. "Nothin' like an ice-cold Co-Cola when it gets hot like this. One'a these days I'm gonna have to get me one of them air conditioners. But that's not what you came out here for." He sat forward, showing way too much male cleavage. "You folks want to know who's doing all the shootin', doncha?" Calvin wiped his mouth on his arm.

So much for Liza's idea of subtle questioning. "Yes, we do want to get some information about the shooting incidents."

"Well, little lady, you came to the right place, at least for part of it. One of my flock came to me not too long ago. Seems he was worried about the police gettin' involved. He's on parole, ya know, and he doesn't want to go back to jail. All he was trying to do was protect the still he has out near the bayou. That night watchman fella got a mite too close for comfort."

That explained the first shooting, but it didn't explain any of the other events.

"Do you honestly believe that was the only time he shot at someone out here?"

"Yes, ma'am. He's a good Christian fella, and if says he only shot at one guy, then he only shot at one guy. Besides, he's moved his still, so you don't have to worry none about him. There's something else I'll bet you folks would like to know. This one's just a rumor that I heard from another church member. His cousin's gone and got hisself involved in something bad, really bad." Calvin frowned. "The cousin's never been too bright, and he might have stumbled into something that'll help him get acquainted with Old Sparky." He was referring to the electric chair.

"What?" Zack's ears perked up.

"From what I've heard, this cousin has a real profitable weed operation. He's even bought himself a double-wide down at the Florida panhandle. I'm afraid this time he's in way over his head. Someone's blackmailed him into getting involved in those murders. Folks are talking about weirdo environmentalists doin' them, but that ain't the truth. That's what they want folks to think, but there's another agenda. Don't know what it is."

"Terrific," Zack muttered. This was worse than he'd thought. "Why haven't you gone to the police?" he asked, although he suspected he already knew the answer.

"I don't trust no po-lice." Calvin drew the word out into two long syllables. "If they're stupid enough not to find someone right under their noses, it's not my job to get involved."

"What do you mean, under their noses?"

"Under their noses. According to the rumor, this person's sittin' right there in the county government. Some kind of big dog."

Zack and Liza suppressed groans. "Is it someone in the Sheriff's Department?" Liza asked.

Calvin scratched his underarm. "Nope, don't think so. Can't say for sure, but I don't expect it is." When one of the hounds ambled over and lifted his leg on the chair, Calvin merely grinned. "About that vandalism on your land, I 'spect that if you put up the right incentive, that'd stop, too. Some of our folks have crops, ya know."

Zack scrubbed his face. This was beyond bizarre. "So, if we sign over some acreage on the far edge of the property, our problems would end?" The Norton Development owned the property so it was his decision, but regardless, Zack looked to Liza for agreement.

Brother Turnipseed grinned, displaying a gleaming row of dentures. "I 'magine that's 'bout right."

"Consider it done." Zack stood and extended his hand. "I'm sure you're a man of your word?"

"That's the absolute truth." The preacher grinned again. "I can guarantee some people in my congregation are gonna be right happy."

Zack was about to ask Calvin a few more questions when Liza jumped up.

"Thanks for all your help, Brother Turnipseed. Just one other thing," she said, sidling back toward the pickup. "Do you really have a pit of snakes out here?"

Calvin laughed. "Yes, ma'am, I surely do. But the folks in those big new houses you're plannin' to build won't have to worry none about copperheads or timber rattlers. They're all right back there." He pointed in the direction of the church.

Liza didn't find that comforting in the least.

She threw the keys to Zack, jumped in the cab of the truck and pulled her feet up on the bench seat.

He reached over and tweaked her nose. "There aren't any snakes in the truck."

"You never can tell." Liza tucked her feet more securely under her. "Can you believe what he said about the murders?"

"Stranger things have happened. We have a meeting with the staff in the next couple of days, don't we?"

"Yes, tomorrow. When can we expect the security guy to show up?"

"Any time now. Do you want to be there when I brief him?"

She wouldn't miss it for the world.

They drove several miles in silence, before Liza asked the question that was on both their minds. "Who do you think he was talking about?"

"I don't know. You're more familiar with the players than I am. What's your take?"

"My money would be on a politician. But what would he or she gain?" Liza pursed her lips. "I suppose it could be someone on staff."

"Yeah," he agreed.

"Are we going to go talk to Uncle Dave?"

"We have to." Zack shot her a glance. "We haven't discounted it being someone from his office, have we?"

"No, I suppose not." Liza couldn't believe that a police officer would be involved, but everything about this situation was peculiar. She wanted her life to go back to the same old boring existence she'd had before. But until they put the murderers out of business, that was nothing but a pipe dream.

Chapter Twenty-Eight

When they returned to the office, Zack decided he was hungry. He was looking for a snack when Ruben strolled in and dropped his briefcase on the kitchen table.

"Liza tells me you guys had an interesting talk with our Blackwater Lake neighbors."

"Boy, I'll say. I'm hoping our bribe will solve that problem. But I'm really more interested in his assertion that someone in the county government is responsible for the murders. That's a whole new ballgame," Zack said.

"Personally, I hope he's wrong."

"Yep." Zack rubbed the back of his neck. "If he's right, that gives us an entirely different set of problems."

"Actually, I think we have a more pressing dilemma," Ruben said.

"What?"

Ruben led Zack to the front room and waved toward the window. "That blue car down the street is the one we saw in the parking lot. It's been around a lot lately."

"Are you positive it's the same one?"

"Yeah. It caught my attention because it looks like an undercover cop car and there's always a guy sitting in the driver's seat," Ruben answered.

Zack might have assumed it was one of the Atlanta folks if he hadn't seen the car *before* he'd hired the security firm.

"It's been there for almost an hour. I noticed it when I drove to the bakery and it hasn't moved. Before that, I saw it parked down the street." Ruben pointed in the opposite direction.

Zack knew his arguments would be bogus, but he thought he'd give them a try. "Could it be someone who works around here and moves the car periodically to avoid getting a ticket?"

"Nope."

"Did the guy look familiar?"

"I didn't get close enough to tell. Do you want me to go see?"

"That's a good idea. If you don't know him, we'll go to the sheriff. I realize Dave can't to anything, but at least we'll have a police report filed."

Five minutes later Ruben returned with the news that he didn't recognize the guy, but he'd been able to get a plate number.

"Let's round up Liza and head over to the cop shop." Zack knew it was a wasted trip, but sometimes you had to jump through a few hoops.

Sheriff Dave was out on a call, so a thin woman with sharp, rodentlike features greeted them in the lobby.

"Hey there, Shirley. How are the kids?" Liza asked.

"Pretty fine, all things considered. You know how it is with teenagers. Come on back to my office."

She led them to a small cubicle, grabbing a metal chair along the way. After they were seated, she listened politely, taking a few notes as they spoke. Finally, she shook her head.

"There isn't anything we can do. If the guy's stalking you, we have laws we can use. But he hasn't made any threats. In fact, you're not even sure he's following anyone. We need more concrete evidence before we can act. At this point, we don't have anything to tie him to any crimes."

Zack decided to save Brother Turnipseed's bombshell until Dave returned.

THE TRIO WERE STILL DISCUSSING the mysterious car when they pulled up in front of their office and found a visitor sitting on the porch.

"I wouldn't want to meet that guy in a dark alley," Liza muttered under her breath. She hoped to goodness he was their new security guard and not a hit man.

The man stood as they approached and reached into his pocket for his wallet. "I'm Rocco Thibodeaux. Veronica assigned me to your case."

Zack checked his identification. "Let's go inside."

They quickly got down to the nitty-gritty. Zack explained his role in the situation. He also shared Brother Turnipseed's story.

Rocco paused in his note taking. "So, my primary job will be to watch Mrs. Henderson during the day?"

"I'll be staying out at Belle Meade at night, so you don't have to worry about evenings."

"Did you folks know that someone in a blue car has been following you?"

"Yeah. I've got the license number."

"Great. I'll get someone to run it through the system. In the meantime I'll keep an eye on him."

THE NEXT MORNING, LIZA WAS prepping the technical consultants for the presentation to the county staff meeting. Zack hoped something would catch his interest. It could be an odd word, a gesture or a comment. Anything to provide a fresh lead. It seemed like every day there was a new wrinkle in the investigation. And the mysterious blue car definitely piqued his curiosity.

"You guys have a couple of hours to get lunch," Liza told the consultants. "Meet us at the courthouse at two."

"Word is that G. Harry is planning to attend the meeting," Ruben said, with a wink at Liza.

If looks could kill, Ruben would be a dead man. However, she managed to reply with ladylike dignity. "I'll have to see him sooner or later, so it may as well be now."

When they arrived at the courthouse people were gathered around the conference table in small groups of two and three. Back in San Francisco, Zack had been fairly adept at spotting suspicious characters. Here, in the home of good old boys and steel magnolias, it was an entirely different story.

Gaylon Smith, the county administrator, strolled in almost fifteen minutes behind schedule. Even so, he stopped to chat before taking his seat at the head of the table. He flipped through some papers and rummaged in his briefcase before checking the clock and announcing that the meeting was getting a late start.

"Before we get to all the department reports, let's go ahead with the Blackwater Lake presentation." Gaylon gave Liza a nod. "Are you ready?"

"Yes, we are."

Zack was quite sure Fred Astaire would be rolling over in his grave before this was over.

Chapter Twenty-Nine

All in all, the presentation had been acceptable. Okay, no one had jumped up and down yelling yippee. But they also hadn't brought out the tar and feathers.

The one aspect of Liza's life that wasn't quite copasetic was Mama's meddling. True to her word, Eleanor Westerfield had organized a Friday-night family dinner at the country club, and Zack was the honored guest. And that was the only reason they were at the Magnolia Bluffs Golf and Country Club.

"How did the meeting with the county folks go yesterday?" Maizie asked, bumping Liza away from the mirror with her hip.

"Darn it, you know I hate it when you hog the mirror."

Her sister smirked. "That's why I do it." She'd been doing the same annoying thing since the twins were old enough to realize there *was* a bathroom mirror. Public facilities were fair game, too—even their current setting, the ladies' room.

Liza tried to maneuver Maizie out of the way, but considering their respective sizes, it was a David-and-Goliath situation. "Scoot your buns over. I need to freshen my lipstick. And leave your hair alone—it looks fine. If we don't get back pretty soon, everyone's gonna think we fell in."

Maizie propped a hip against the porcelain sink, sporting a grin that rivaled Dennis Quaid's best.

"I have to know. Are you two doing the horizontal boogie, and is he as good-looking butt-nekkid as he is clothed?"

Liza popped her twin on the arm. "Maizie! That's, that's—" She broke into a fit of giggles. "That's just too much, even for you. And yes, he's ab-so-lute-ly gorgeous. But I'm not telling you anything else!"

Maizie's grin faded. "On a more serious note, what about all the yucky stuff that's been happening? And who is that scary-looking guy sticking to you like glue?"

"He's my bodyguard. Zack hired extra security."

Maizie squealed. "Do you *need* a bodyguard?"

"Possibly. We may be close to solving one of our problems." Liza shook her head. "I don't know about the rest of it, though." Hoping to change the subject, she told Maizie that Charlie was thinking about coming home.

"Really?"

"Yep, he's tired of traveling. Personally, I suspect he's even more tired of hiding."

"You be careful, now, ya hear?"

"I always am," Liza assured her.

Maizie put her lipstick back in her purse. "Here's a segue you're gonna love. You do realize Mama's out there interrogating Zack right this minute."

Lord in heaven! Of course she was. She was incorrigible. That was the one and only reason she'd invited them to the club for dinner.

"Swear to goodness, I'll strangle her with her pearls. Come on." Liza grabbed Maizie's arm. "Let's rescue what's left of my dignity."

Liza made it back to the table just in time to hear her mother—in her oh-so-subtle Miss Melanie way—ask Zack about his finances. She would never have been so gauche as to outright ask how much he made. She preferred the "peck 'em to death" method. And knowing Mama, the earlier questions were probably about his marriageability, his medical history and his pedigree.

"Is it too late to be an orphan?" Liza whispered.

"Yes, ma'am. It's way too late for that," Maizie replied.

The next question concerned Zack's mother's volunteer activity. Yep—Mama was in full pecking mode. In her world, ladies didn't work. They simply volunteered themselves silly. Fortunately, Liza and Maizie had ignored that lesson.

"Did you know that Liza's silver pattern is Grand Baroque?"

Not the silver-pattern discussion!

Zack grinned. "Really?"

The poor man didn't know that talking about silver patterns was the precursor to booking a church and reserving the country-club ballroom for an intimate but lavish reception.

Time to nip it in the bud. "Mama, I have sterling-silver iced-tea spoons for thirty-six, and Zack's not interested in that, either."

It was a valiant effort, but it would take a howitzer to stop Eleanor Westerfield when she was on a roll. "Did you also know that Liza had her coming-out in a lovely ball in Atlanta? Lordy, my two girls were the prettiest debs ever." Eleanor fanned herself. "Liza was pretty as a picture. Swear to goodness, I was so proud."

"Mama!"

Zack looked as if he wanted to chuckle, but his mother obviously hadn't raised a fool. "A debutante, huh?" He squeezed Liza's hand under the table.

"Don't you dare laugh," she muttered.

"Mama, it's been lovely, but we have to go." Liza kissed Eleanor's cheek and gave her dad a big hug. "We have a long day tomorrow. And you—" She turned to Maizie. "I'll talk to you later. I have something important to ask you."

Her twin smiled her best Miss Central Georgia smile.

On the way out to the car, Zack pulled Liza behind a magnolia and kissed her socks off. "Grand Baroque? Is that supposed to mean something?"

"It means my mother is nutty and I have enough silver for the entire Russian army."

He had no idea just how close he'd come to the altar. In this case, ignorance was bliss, at least for Zack.

Chapter Thirty

Before Zack went to work the next morning, he made a detour by the sheriff's office. Dave Madison was blown away by Brother Turnipseed's revelation. He wasn't quite convinced it was true, but he quickly agreed to do a thorough investigation. With that chore out of the way, Zack ran by the bakery for some goodies and then headed back to the office.

Uh-oh! Liza looked as if she was in the mood to kick ass and take names. When he'd left home she'd been fine. So what had happened?

She thrust a pile of sticky notes at him. "I'm not your secretary."

He put his hands up in surrender. "Whoa. What's the deal?" He pulled one of the sheets out of the pile. Angela had called—apparently more than once. How in the world had she found him?

He crumpled the papers and tossed them in the trash can. "If she phones again, please tell her I died."

"Humph! I'll tell her more than that if I have to talk to her again." Liza stalked to her office.

Another Angela victim. He had enough on his plate without worrying about what that she-cat was planning. Right now he needed to think about the call he'd received from Bambi, the county planner, requesting a private meeting. What did she want? Could she be up to something nefarious?

"I'm heading out to run some errands."

Considering Liza's current mood, he was pretty sure he could have been going to the moon and she wouldn't give a flying fig.

The same fashion-impaired woman was at the desk at the planning department when he arrived.

"Hi, I have a meeting with Bambi."

"I'll tell her you're here," she said without looking up. "Go on down to the Kudzu room. It's the first door on your right."

Zack followed her directions and took a chair with his back to the wall. He might be paranoid, but at this point, he didn't trust anyone.

Bambi strolled into the room a few minutes later, hips swaying. "I'm glad you came. We haven't had much chance to talk privately, have we?" She ignored the empty chairs and circled the table to sit next to him.

That woman had to have a closet full of ugly clothing. This time she was in full matador regalia, complete with a swirling red cape and a small circular hat atop her mass of blond curls.

The hair stood up on the back of his neck. She was a female barracuda, out for blood.

The man-eater leaned toward him, carefully positioning her crimson-tipped acrylic nails on his leg. "Honey, we've been needin' to talk. You know what I mean." She flipped the cape open to reveal a skintight black leotard.

Oh yeah, he knew what she meant. Opting to appear obtuse, he muttered, "No, I'm not sure I understand. Why don't you sit down and we can talk."

She waved a hand, dismissing his suggestion. "Meet me at the Dew Drop Inn tavern at eight o'clock tonight. I'll share a few of my ideas about how we can help each other. You can't miss it. It's down on Benton Street. It usually has a bunch of Harleys parked out front. Don't disappoint me." She leaned back in the chair as if nothing out of the ordinary had happened.

"WHAT DO YOU MEAN SHE WANTS to meet you at the Dew Drop Inn?" Liza screeched when he got back to the office and told her what had happened. "She's reprehensible. What does she want?"

Zack exchanged glances with Ruben before responding. "I think she's going to proposition me, and I need to find out what she wants in exchange."

"If you insist on meeting her, take Ruben with you."

"I can take care of myself. I'll give her thirty minutes, then I'm out of there. That'll give me long enough to find out what she's up to." Zack cupped Liza's chin. "I promise nothing bad will happen to me. I know martial arts."

"I don't think you'd have a chance in hell of throwing her," Ruben tossed. "But if it'll make Liza feel better, I'll go with you and stay in the car. How about that, cupcake?"

"That *would* make me feel better," she answered.

"YOU'RE WAY TOO CLEAN." Ruben eyed Zack's T-shirt and jeans disdainfully. "The folks who go to that dump aren't exactly the classiest bunch. Take my advice. Order a beer, see what Bambi's up to and then get out."

"Yes, Daddy, I got it. And I won't ask for a microbrew, either." Zack had pulled more undercover stints than Ruben could even imagine. And he'd been inside dives far worse than the Dew Drop Inn.

Ruben pulled into an empty spot half a block away from a group of motorcycles and cut the engine. "There's probably more to this situation than a simple seduction. But I guess we'll see. Now, go get 'em. I'll be parked right here."

The aroma of stale beer and sweat was familiar—not pleasant, not welcome, simply familiar. Zack strolled through the tavern, waiting for his eyes to adjust. Patience was the key to survival— that and the semiautomatic strapped to his ankle. A quick reconnaissance revealed a couple of bikers playing pool at the back of the room and three seedy characters occupying the bar stools. A muted TV above the bar was tuned to a Braves game.

"A Bud, no glass," he barked to the husky bartender.

He scarcely had time to wipe the top of the can before Bambi emerged from the dimly lit recesses of the tavern. Wearing skin-tight jeans and a fringed cowboy shirt, she blended into the environment like a chameleon.

She stroked his arm and purred, "We're in the back. It's a little more private." Hooking her thumb in his belt loop, she steered him to the darkest corner of the bar. So much for his seduction theory. The "we" blew that right out of the water.

Bambi motioned to the table and draped herself around a bespectacled man. "You remember Sam Coleson, our senior inspector."

"Yes, of course. How are you, Sam?" This certainly wasn't playing out the way he'd expected. "Can we get down to the reason for this meeting? I get the feeling it isn't purely social."

"Zack, it's like this." Bambi leaned forward to display her ample cleavage. "Sam and I hold the fate of your project in our hands. If I write a bad recommendation, or utter a word of doubt to one of our county supervisors, poof, there it goes." She fluttered her fingers. "That's at the planning level. Then for the sake of argument, let's say you get through that phase. There's always the construction inspection. That's where Sammy comes in. His guys can put a stop-work order on you like that." She snapped her fingers. "These scenarios are just theoretical, you understand. We want to make sure you properly appreciate us." Bambi smiled as she ran her fingertip down Sam's cheek.

This was a curveball. He had come in expecting a proposition. Instead he was being threatened.

Bambi turned her attention to Zack. "I wouldn't want you to get the wrong idea. If we're going to be friends, we need to agree to help each other. That's why we asked you to join us. Sam and I are buying a house, but we have a little cash-flow problem.

It would certainly be *helpful* to have, say, fifty thousand for a down payment. A loan, of course."

"Does that fifty thousand guarantee me anything specific, or does it just provide smooth sailing?" They didn't even notice his barely veiled sarcasm.

"I'm sure we can work out an arrangement that will make us all happy. Right, Sammy?" Bambi said.

"I need to talk to my boss before I commit that kind of money. I'll get back to you soon." Zack stood and headed to the door.

"You're not going to believe this," he exploded once he got in Ruben's car. "Bambi had Sam Coleson with her. She didn't want to jump my bones. They want a fifty-thousand-dollar 'loan.' And if I don't provide it, they said things could get tough for us, in both the planning and the construction phases."

"Son of a—! I've heard rumors, but I didn't believe them. Guess we have to tell Liza, huh?"

That wouldn't be Zack's first choice. "She doesn't own a gun, does she?"

Ruben laughed as he sped toward the office. Zack noticed that he didn't answer the question.

LIZA PACED THE OFFICE reception area. "The witch wants a no-interest, no-payment loan, or she and that obsequious little nerd will stop the development. I can't believe this! How does that ostentatious, silicone-augmented floozy think she'll get away with this?" She continued to rant as she paced.

Liza finally whirled to a stop. "We have to talk to the county supervisors, and let them know what's happening." She rubbed her forehead. "We could go to the planning director, but I'm not sure that's the right way to handle this."

Ruben nodded. "I suspect you need to speak to the county administrator. If that doesn't work, you can talk to each of the supervisors separately." He turned to Zack. "You may have to meet with Bambi and Sam again. But this time carry a tape recorder. This business is hard enough without having to deal with this kind of crap."

Zack couldn't agree more. "We also have to consider the fact that if they're willing to stoop to extortion, they might be capable of murder."

Chapter Thirty-One

The next day, Liza was still trying to get a handle on the latest complication. As usual, when things got dicey, it was time to call in the reinforcements—Maizie and Kenni. True to form, Maizie jumped at the chance to play hooky.

Liza phoned Kenni next. "Hey, girl. What are you doing?"

"I'm waiting for a color job to process, but I'll be finished in about thirty minutes. What's up?"

"I need some advice, and probably a little bit of help. Can you meet us at the Coffee Cup in an hour?"

"I wouldn't miss it for the world."

That was the start of the Three Musketeers' next foray into sleuthing.

IT WAS BARELY DARK when Liza pulled into Maizie's drive and flashed her high beams. It was the signal for her buddies to get their butts outside, ASAP. They had things to do and places to go.

Ditching Zack and her babysitter hadn't been easy, but Liza was resourceful. Zack followed her to Mama's house, but left her there when she promised to call him when she was ready to leave.

The twins had been friends with Mary Rutherford Hawkins since their first day at the Little Daisy Camp. Mary also happened to be the county clerk. She had access to every office in the courthouse, including G. Harry's, so it was off to the courthouse.

Liza took one look at Maizie's Laura Ashley dress and sneered. "I didn't know we were going to a garden party."

"At least it's more professional than that." Maizie waved a hand at Liza's capris and oversize T-shirt.

Kenni wisely stayed out of the sisters' discussion of the proper attire for a felony. "Mary will be waiting for us at the front door. Right?" she asked.

"Yep," Maizie answered. "She told me that the cleaning crew doesn't come on until nine, so we have plenty of time." She started to chew on a nail but caught herself. "I can't believe I got talked into another dumb scheme. This technically could be construed as breaking and entering. If we get busted, we'll wind up in jail. Even Uncle Dave won't be able to save us."

"We won't get caught," Liza said with a long-suffering sigh. "All I want to do is check his computer for anything incriminating. Besides, we're not breaking, we're just entering."

Kenni broke into giggles, eliciting a matching chuckle from Maizie.

True to her word, Mary was waiting at the front door. She shooed them inside the minute they arrived. As innocent as Mary looked, she was always ready to misbehave.

"Come on. Let's get this show on the road. I have his computer all booted up and," she said with a suggestive eyebrow waggle, "I even found his password." Mary waved a piece of paper in the air. "Can you believe it? He had it taped to the bottom of his desk drawer. The man is *not* a rocket scientist. I hope you find something juicy enough to get him recalled."

Before she left, Mary gave them a few final instructions. "You have thirty minutes until the cleaning crew starts. I'll be your lookout. I have his office number on my cell. If the phone rings, get out of here, fast. And whatever you do, don't leave any trace that you've been messing around on his computer."

"Yes, ma'am." Liza gave her a salute and sat down at the desk.

She wasn't a hacker, but with the password, this should be easy. Then she opened the first picture.

"Yeech!"

"Ew!" Maizie and Kenni squealed in unison. "How are they doing that?"

Liza clicked off the graphic and went to a Word file. By the end of their thirty minutes, they'd found a ton of bookmarked porn sites. In the Bible Belt, that was enough to blast G. Harry's political career all the way to Mexico. Unfortunately, they didn't find any indication that he was involved in the murders.

Liza flicked the hair out of her face. "Just because we couldn't find a smoking gun doesn't mean he didn't do it." She prepared to shut down the unit.

"One thing's for sure, he's a sicko," Maizie said.

Liza shrugged. "That's one of the reasons I want him gone."

But, if G. Harry wasn't the perp, who was it?

Chapter Thirty-Two

Liza and her coconspirators agreed the adventure would be their secret. Zack would have a fit if he found out what they'd done, and there was no telling what the husbands would do.

So how could she slip him the info about G. Harry?

She was trying to multitask—cooking while simultaneously pondering her situation—but the man nibbling on her neck was a huge distraction.

"I set up a meeting with the county administrator tomorrow morning at nine," Zack said. "I didn't give him *all* the gory details, just enough so that he almost had a coronary. I'll bet he's on the phone to the county attorney as we speak."

Liza swatted him as he started a new onslaught of kisses. Darn the man. How could he talk business when she couldn't breathe? "I can't chop these carrots while you're doing that."

Zack turned his attention to her earlobe. "I'm sure Bambi and Sam are going to find themselves in big trouble. In a private organization, they wouldn't last five minutes with that kind of crap."

His earlobe technique was beyond delicious. "Yeah, well, that's the private sector. In the public sector, there's a perverted tendency to protect the employees, even if they are scumbags."

He laid a finger against her lips. "Shh. I have other plans for that sassy mouth of yours."

Zack had barely uttered the suggestion when the doorbell rang.

"Who could that be?" Liza asked rhetorically. "Only my family has the code for the gate. And they would've called to tell me they were coming."

"Why don't you stand back and let me see," Zack said.

He checked the peephole, and when he turned she knew it was bad. "Liza—"

He wasn't able to finish his sentence before there was insistent knocking on the door.

"Honey, it's your mother."

Mama? The Eleanor Westerfield she knew and loved would never make a surprise visit.

Liza jerked the door open. There stood Mama and Daddy, Maizie and Clay, Kenni and Win, Aunt Anna Belle and Uncle Joe, Cassie and Jim and Uncle Dave and Aunt Eugenie. The only family members missing were Kara and Maizie's hound dog.

"What!" Liza exclaimed. Zack appeared to be as bewildered as she was.

Uncle Dave took the initiative. "Liza, sweetie, why don't you let us come in."

Liza finally realized she was blocking the entrance. "Sure, come on in." Then her shock subsided enough to realize something truly horrific must have happened. "Oh, no! Not Kara."

Maizie was the first to react. She reached for Liza's hands. "No, no. Kara's fine. She'll be here shortly."

"Then what?"

"I need to talk to you." Uncle Dave was wearing his cop face. That wasn't a good omen.

He sat down on the couch and patted the cushion next to him. "Come on."

The rest of the family looked as if they'd rather be anywhere else.

Liza complied, pulling Zack down beside her. "What?"

"Um, you know that we're widening the county road to your house."

"Yeah." What did that have to do with her?

"Well, they had to cut down some trees and clear out the kudzu."

Oh, no! She felt her heart beat faster.

"Up around that bad curve, we found a car," Dave said, twirling his hat the way he did when he was nervous.

"A car? You mean someone drove off and no one ever found them?"

The pieces were beginning to fall into place. If Zack's expression was any indication, he also knew what was coming. But, it wouldn't be true until someone uttered the words.

"It's Rob's car, honey. We've sent the, uh, body to the medical examiner in Atlanta for identification."

Liza collapsed against the sofa cushion, feeling the pain of Rob's disappearance all over again. Her heart had told her that one day this would happen. But, still—

Her girls needed her to be strong.

Cassie left her husband's embrace and walked into her mother's arms. The two women found strength in each other, and when Kara arrived they enfolded her in the family hug.

Her daughters frequently seemed so grown-up. On rare occasions they reverted to their childhood, but now they assumed the role of comforters.

The family plied them with coffee, bourbon, hugs and lots of TLC. Finally, Liza was desperate for peace and quiet. With everyone around, it was impossible to process her thoughts.

"Sweetheart, will you be okay?" she asked Cassie.

"I'm fine. In fact, I think Jim and I need to go home. We left the boys with a babysitter."

"I love you all, really I do, but I'm ready for everyone to go home," Liza announced to the group.

"I'll be glad to spend the night," Maizie offered.

"Thanks, but no. I'll be fine." Liza felt oddly detached from the situation—more like an observer. It had to be the shock, and when it wore off, she wasn't sure exactly what she'd feel.

Closure.

Anguish.

Relief that Rob hadn't deserted them.

Probably all of the above.

"Come on, Eleanor." Daddy pushed Mama toward the door. "Sweetie, we'll call you in the morning." He paused to give Liza a kiss before escorting Mama and the aunts out.

Kara said she was exhausted and went up to her own room. Zack was the only person left, and he was making his way toward the exit.

"*Everyone* did not mean you."

He looked surprised. "Do you want me to stay?"

"I want you to hold me."

Without a word, he wrapped her in his arms.

Chapter Twenty-Three

The next three weeks passed in a blur of condolences, family visits and preparation for the memorial service. Liza worked herself to exhaustion. Intellectually, she realized she was trying to obliterate thoughts of what might have been. Everything not directly associated with her family had fallen by the wayside. But her heart told her that now she had the freedom to contemplate her future.

Kara returned to school. Cassie was busy with her family. And most of the other relatives had resumed their normal activities. For them, life continued with its normal cadence. And Liza was determined to join them.

Zack was at her side the entire time. He comforted her, he held her when she needed it most, he encouraged her and he managed all the details. He was her rock, and she fell more and more in love with him every day.

"WE'VE PUT OFF DEALING with this Bambi business long enough," Liza announced one Sunday morning as they lingered over a second cup of coffee.

Zack looked up from the sports section. "You don't have to worry about any of that. I'll take care of it."

"It's time for me to get back to work."

"If that's what you want to do, I'm with you." He graced her with one of his sexiest grins. "I can certainly use your help."

"Tomorrow, I'll make an appointment with the county administrator. For today, I have other ideas," she said. After weeks of putting her emotions on ice, her libido was thawing like a river in late spring. "What do you think about taking the paper and spending the morning in bed?"

"Reading?"

"Not exactly."

It was amazing how fast a guy could run up the stairs.

WEDNESDAY MORNING, THEY WERE sitting outside the county administrator's office. It was almost an hour past their scheduled appointment time. Liza had read *People* magazine twice, and nursed several cups of stale coffee. To make matters worse she'd had to kick Zack whenever he muttered a disparaging remark about bureaucrats—which he did more frequently the longer they waited.

"Mr. Smith will see you now," the receptionist said, standing to lead them to the administrator's conference room.

"I hope this isn't a sign of how our meeting's going to go," she whispered.

Several people were already seated. Zack recognized Gaylon Smith and Trevor Creekmore. He didn't know the middle-aged Hispanic man or the elegant Asian woman in a severe black suit.

The woman quickly rectified that situation. "I'm Alana Chen, the county attorney. This is Eric Hernandez, the assistant county administrator. I believe you know everyone else. Please have a seat. I'm sure we'll find a solution that will be acceptable for everyone involved."

Zack wasn't positive about the "everyone involved" part, but he decided to play along. He nodded and smiled as he and Liza took their places at the table.

"I know you can appreciate our position." The attorney's colleagues could have been carved from stone. They didn't move, they didn't smile and they didn't speak.

"We're faced with an unsubstantiated accusation against two

people who have been exemplary employees for several years. In the interest of fairness, I suggest we create a hypothetical scenario. Let's say these employees have been highly critical of your project. And that you would have quite a bit to gain if—and this is certainly a big if, because I would never accuse you of anything—but if these employees were taken off your project. You can see our dilemma."

Her smile was approaching a sneer.

Trevor Creekmore appeared inordinately interested in the contents of his coffee mug.

"Ms. Chen, I'm sure you weren't suggesting we're making a false accusation. Although that certainly was how it sounded." Liza glared at the men sitting across the table. "I can assure you that we want to settle this equitably. But if the county allows these two individuals to continue working on our project, we will immediately seek other remedies—either political or legal." She stared at Alana Chen. "What is your proposition?"

Ms. Chen wrapped her disdain around herself like a Kevlar cape. "As I said before, the accusations are unsubstantiated." She paused. "So we're proposing to give the project responsibility to Trevor Creekmore. Bambi and Sam will remain on the job, but they'll report to him."

"That's absolutely unacceptable." Liza picked up her briefcase. "I suspect this isn't the first time they've pulled this stunt. But I personally intend to make it their last. And if you collectively, or individually, have knowledge of prior incidents, I *will* hold you responsible."

Zack followed along in her wake as she swept out of the conference room. He waited until they were alone in the elevator before hazarding a glance in her direction.

To his surprise, Liza smiled. "All in all, I think that went well, don't you?" She broke into laughter at the look on his face. "I've had battles with her before. If you give her an inch, she'll take ten miles. We have to be firm. Besides, I'll bet Ruben can find others who've had to bribe Bambi and Sam. We can take our evidence to either the politicos or the press. Hardball is the only thing these people understand, and that's the game we have to play. Don't worry. We'll win in the end." She pinched his cheek as the elevator doors opened. "But on a completely different topic, remember, you're taking me to that darned wedding tomorrow night. I can't believe I agreed to participate in the atrocity. But how can you say no to Vivian? I assumed they'd get someone else, but they didn't. So, I'm stuck."

"Your enthusiasm is overwhelming." Actually, he was delighted she was feisty enough to gripe about hoopskirts, pink nuptials and Southern belles.

Chapter Thirty-Four

Liza tried to pull up the bodice of the pink satin bridesmaid dress. Up, down—shoot, nothing was going to make the abomination any better. It looked fine on Maizie, but she had the cleavage to make it work. Liza, on the other hand, felt like she was playing dress-up in one of Mama's ball gowns.

And that hoopskirt! It was impossible to get through a door without flashing everyone in sight, and now she was knocking stuff off tables. The other bridesmaids seemed to be managing fine. However, if she remembered correctly, they were all Kappa Delta Thetas. They'd been trained for this stuff since they were toddlers.

The wedding coordinator stuck her head in the door. "Are you ladies ready?"

The sooner they marched down the aisle, the sooner she could ditch the *Gone with the Wind* duds. "Sure, let's go." Liza was the first out the door and down the aisle.

THE RECEIVING LINE WAS ALREADY forming by the time the bridesmaids' limo arrived at the country club after the ceremony. Sitting and standing were still a chore, but doors were the biggest challenge of all. "When can I get out of this contraption?" Liza asked as Maizie pranced by.

"Not till after the first dance."

"When is that?"

"After dinner."

"You mean I have to eat in this getup?" No. Tell her it wasn't so.

Maizie laughed. "Yep. And did I mention the wedding pictures?"

"Wedding pictures?" Liza shot her twin her best gimlet eye, but Maizie wasn't fazed.

"Amen, sister. You're about to be featured in Viv's wedding hall of fame."

Liza had totally forgotten about the wedding pictures. She was about to utter an expletive that would blister the ears of a Dixie Belle when she caught sight of Zack. Lord, the man looked lost. And no wonder. He probably thought he was stuck in the middle of a strawberry milkshake.

She took his arm. "I could use a drink."

"Done." He grabbed two flutes of champagne as a waiter walked by. "Let's hide in the corner. That way you can chug it."

Liza drained the glass in one huge gulp and gave a very un-belle-like burp. "Okay, now I can face that." She waved her hand in the direction of eleven—count 'em, eleven—middle-aged women in pink satin hoopskirts. Unfortunately, she made an even dozen.

"Why don't you go on into the ballroom and find our table? The place cards are, as you can probably guess, pink." Champagne made her as giggly as a schoolgirl. "I need to hit the ladies' room. We have hours of toasts coming up." She only hoped she'd be able to wedge her skirt into one of the stalls.

"Hurry back."

"Don't worry, no one will bite. Maizie, take care of him for me."

"Sure. Clay, would you talk sports with Zack while I gossip with Mama?" Maizie said.

Liza wandered down the hall toward the restrooms, reflecting on how ridiculous this experience had been. A middle-aged woman with four marriages under her belt should have the decency to elope.

"Hello, Liza."

"Hi, Helen." Helen Damon was related to the groom, so it wasn't surprising that she'd attend the wedding. "We really enjoyed our lunch with you."

"How is your handsome associate?" Helen asked.

"He's great." Not sure what else to say, Liza left it at that.

"When is he planning to go back to California?"

"I…don't know." Why was she asking?

"Does he have much control over how the project is run?"

"Yes." Liza wasn't about to share Zack's true position in the company. However, she didn't see any reason to equivocate about his authority. "He's quite influential."

"Really? I would like to know if he plans to be here throughout the entire permitting process. Would you ask him and get back to me?"

"Yeah…well, sure." Although men did deals in bars all the time, Liza found conducting business in the ladies' room a bit disconcerting. In fact, there was something off-putting about the entire exchange, though she couldn't quite put her finger on what it was.

Zack left his discussion of the Braves when Liza returned. "Let's find our table," he suggested.

"Guess who I talked to in the restroom?"

"A woman, I hope."

Liza gave him a playful jab. "Helen Damon. It was strange. She was digging for information about you."

"Me?"

"You."

"Why?"

Liza shrugged. "Beats me. I usually don't do business dressed like this, so I was distracted."

THE HELEN EPISODE WAS QUICKLY forgotten as the festivities progressed with the traditional dinner, toasts, cake cutting and first dance.

"I had a good time," Zack said as they walked out to the car when it was all over. "Your parents cut a mean rug."

"They do, don't they? As much as I hate to admit it, I had fun. But if I ever get married again, I swear to God I'm having a picnic."

Now that was an interesting subject. Was she ready to discuss marriage? Only time would tell. Lately, he'd been seriously considering making a life with Liza in Magnolia Bluffs. But he had to be patient. It was a good thing he was a veteran of stakeouts and perseverance.

He couldn't get close to Liza without her hoopskirt flipping up over her head, so kissing in the parking lot was obviously out. When they got home, all bets were off.

Chapter Thirty-Five

From the moment Zack came to Magnolia Bluffs, Liza's life had been turned upside down. She'd been shot at twice, nearly been kidnapped and her status had changed from deserted wife to widow. Even more disconcerting was the fact she was in love with a man who would eventually leave.

What should she do? That was a no-brainer. It was time to call in the cavalry.

"Maizie, I'm having an emergency. Meet me at the bakery." She left an identical message at the salon with Raylene, one of Kenni's stylists.

Maizie had the nerve to laugh when she called back. "Need something gooey and sweet, do you? You're in luck, Sally can take over. I'll be there in five minutes."

As usual, Maizie was dressed to the nines when she joined Liza at the table in the bakery. Hair, makeup, jewelry—the only accessory she was missing was hosiery.

Maizie fluttered her beringed fingers at Liza. "Mama would have a fit if she saw you out in public dressed like that."

"And what's wrong with my clothes?" She was perfectly happy in her cargo shorts and tank top. "I'm not going to the office or I'd dress up. Zack likes me the way I am. That's the problem."

Maizie pulled out her wallet. "Zack's a problem? And do you want anything else?" She glanced at the Napoleon and chocolate doughnut already on Liza's plate. "How about you?" she asked Liza's bodyguard at the next table.

The bodyguard shook his head, but Liza wasn't so reserved. "No, I don't want anything else. And I'm not talking to you until you get some sugar in that smart mouth of yours."

Maizie returned with her pastry just as Kenni arrived. "Hey, guys. What's up? Raylene didn't tell me much."

"Liza's having a chocolate crisis," Maizie replied, biting into her apple fritter.

"That bad, huh?"

"Yep." Maizie turned her attention to her sister. "Okay, we're here. Spill your guts."

Liza put her head in her hands. Why in the world had she thought they could help? She looked at her bodyguard to see if he was listening. Thankfully, he was paying more attention to his breakfast than to their conversation.

"Having people in my hip pocket 24-7 is making me crazy. I feel like the First Lady. But I have to admit, I'm scared. So much has happened in the past couple of weeks. All of a sudden it hit me. Someone still wants to hurt me."

Maizie patted her hand. "We're glad everyone's keeping you safe." She put her arms around her sister. "They'll find out who's responsible for this craziness. You wait and see."

Liza shrugged, hoping that was true. "Uncle Dave's working hard, but so far, they haven't found anything useful." She leaned forward to whisper, "We need to take matters into our own hands."

Maizie stared at her for a few seconds, and then guffawed. "We tried that before, remember? We were terrible!"

"I don't mean slinking around in the middle of the night. I think the Magnolia Bluffs rumor mill is the key. It's better than the FBI."

Maizie's eyes bugged out. "You don't mean Laverne Hightower, do you?"

"Wow, I should have suggested that!" Kenni exclaimed.

Miss Hightower had been instrumental in solving the death of Aunt Hallie Rule back when Kenni and Win were dating. "I'll never forget taking Win out to her house. The way she fawned all over him, I couldn't decide if she was going to adopt him or marry him."

"If he wasn't already taken, I'd be interested," Maizie said with a sly grin. "He's a fine man."

"Ladies, let's get back to Miss Hightower," Liza said, interrupting. When Maizie and Kenni wandered off on a tangent, it was nearly impossible to get them back to the original subject. "I want you both to go out there with me." *That* got their attention.

Laverne Hightower knew everything about everyone.

"I already called her and she's expecting us in an hour."

"Wonderful, I can't wait." Maizie's dull tone contradicted her words of enthusiasm.

"You need to control your sarcasm, sister."

"Whatever. If I have to go to Miss Hightower's place, you have to pay me back with some info. Inquiring minds want to know how you and Zack are getting along. We've all noticed he hasn't left your side for the past three weeks."

"Officially, he sleeps in the guest room."

"Officially?" Kenni winked.

"That's for Mama's consumption," Maizie answered. "The way he looks at Liza gives me goose bumps." She rubbed her arms in a mock display of chills. "It's obvious he's smitten."

"So am I," Liza admitted reluctantly. "And that's what worries me. I think I'm in love with him. I'm not wired for a casual affair and he's not going to stay. He has a job, and a life, in the big city. Our little burg can't compete with that. And I can't stand any more heartache, not after Rob."

Maizie grew more serious. "So how does he feel about you?"

"I know he likes me. And although he hasn't actually said it, I think he loves me. But he also has a ton of issues from his first marriage. What a mess." And she couldn't blame anyone but herself.

"Uh-oh. Speaking of Mr. Trouble, here he comes."

Zack was barreling toward to their table. "Ladies, may I join you?"

Maizie and Kenni immediately said yes.

He nudged Liza's leg to get her to make room. "Sweetheart, scoot over."

He was too big, too overpowering and too sexy by far. Things were in such a tangle, and all she could think about was hauling him back to the house for a "nap." She was a nymphomaniac; that had to be the problem.

Zack ordered a cup of coffee and when the waitress left, he got down to business. "I have some news about the guy in the blue car. He's a private investigator from Atlanta. I'm not sure who he's working for, but there's no obvious local connection."

"What!" Liza squeaked. "So, why's he following us?"

"I don't know, but I intend to find out. I thought working in the Tenderloin district was weird, but we didn't have moonshiners and snake handlers. And now there's this mysterious private eye. At least he doesn't seem to be dangerous."

Liza was trying to wrap her mind around this latest turn of events, but decided she'd better tell Zack about her plan.

"I have this idea. As you know, the Magnolia Bluffs grapevine is incredibly efficient. And Miss Laverne Hightower is our local rumor monger. We decided we'd go out to visit her this afternoon to see what we can find out."

"You weren't planning to invite me, were you?"

"Um…"

"That's what I thought." Zack glared at her. "You're not going anywhere without me."

Lord, that man was stubborn.

LIZA OPENED THE CREAKY GATE of the white picket fence and led their group up a path overgrown with vines and trailing roses. "Let me warn you, Miss Laverne is a bit eccentric."

That wasn't encouraging. Almost everyone he'd met since his arrival was peculiar, and yet, this was the first one he'd been warned about.

The woman who answered their knock looked like an apple doll with a scrunched-up face.

"Hi there, Miss Laverne. This is my friend Zack Maynard. I told you about him," Liza said cheerfully.

The old woman appeared frail, but in this case, looks were deceiving. With an amazingly strong grip, she grabbed Zack's arm and yanked him inside. "It's always nice to have a gentleman caller. Come in. I've made some fresh lemonade."

Maizie and Kenni rolled their eyes.

"Ever feel like a third wheel?" Maizie whispered.

After what seemed like an interminable session of lemonade and sugar cookies, Liza finally managed to draw the conversation back to the questions at hand.

"Miss Laverne, we'd like to ask you something. It's really important."

The older woman gave Zack a coquettish smile. "You name it."

"We need some information on the folks in county government. Anything you know about the board of supervisors, the county administrator or the department heads would be helpful."

Miss Laverne paused. "Well, I'm not one to tell tales, but did you know that G. Harry Middleton has been married multiple times to the same woman? Mercy, that girl was stupid. She finally smartened up and skedaddled off to her family in Florida."

That *was* new, but poor marriage choices wouldn't make a killer.

"What about Leonard Dunwoodie?"

Miss Laverne tapped her fingernail on her front teeth. "Let's see, his daddy's a preacher."

"And…"

"And you know what they say about preachers' kids." She cackled. "Seems there was something odd about his brother. Or was that his sister? I can't remember much about it."

Zack took the opportunity to jump into the conversation. "What about the department heads?"

"The sheriff's clean as a whistle. But you girls know that. Trevor Creekmore, the planning fellow, got arrested when he was a kid. Drugs, I believe. I can't quite recall the details on that one, either."

While she continued her narrative of petty shoplifting, who was sleeping with whom and who had a misdemeanor record, Zack let his mind wander. Okay, they had a juvenile druggie, a preacher's kid, a philanderer and a pervert. Nice!

"And then there's Helen Damon. The hippie lady. She grew up in Atlanta, but she has family here. I heard that when her brother died, she went over the edge."

Zack remembered Liza mentioning her comment about a twin. "What happened to him?"

Miss Laverne pursed her lips. "I'm not rightly sure. I'll have to think on that one."

"Is there anyone else on the staff who might be interesting?"

Laverne waggled her fingers dismissively. "They're not from around here."

Zack wasn't quite sure what that meant, but he'd just lump them into his mental category labeled Aliens. Unfortunately, that term also described him to a T. Although he was considering staying in Magnolia Bluffs, he wasn't sure he'd ever fit in. Kenni's husband seemed to have made the transition. A conversation with Win was in order, but Zack's first priority was keeping Liza safe.

Chapter Thirty-Six

The trip to Miss Hightower's house hadn't yielded much. The investigation was stalled, and Zack was afraid it was up to him to jump-start it.

He rolled over to watch Liza sleep in the early morning light. In the short while he'd known her, she'd become very important to him. After his marriage, he'd been hesitant to even consider love. In this case, though, he was ready, willing and able.

They hadn't gotten much sleep last night, and it wasn't from insomnia. He gently ran his finger down Liza's cheek, careful not to wake her.

"Shh, quiet," he whispered to the dogs as he rolled out of bed. P.B. cracked an eye, obviously deciding it was too early to get up. Jelly yawned, made a doggy circle before settling down again.

Zack was brewing a pot of coffee when his cell phone rang.

"Maynard here," he answered.

"Mr. Maynard, this is G. Harry Middleton. Would it be possible for you to meet me tomorrow? Say, five o'clock at my office. I have something I want to discuss with you."

"Okay, I'll be there."

"By the way, don't tell anyone," G. Harry said and hung up without bothering with social niceties.

What was that all about?

Before Zack could fill his mug, his cell rang again. Helen

Damon invited him to come by her office at seven o'clock that evening. She said she was upset about the Bambi episode and wanted to discuss it with him. Interestingly, she asked that he keep this meeting secret, too.

So much for a caffeine fix. He might as well go back to bed. He couldn't think of a better use for the day than lounging around with the prettiest girl in Georgia.

"Hey, cutie. You want to play? The big bad wolf is here."

Zack watched Liza's eyelids flicker as his voice roused her from sleep. God, she was adorable in the morning. Dried drool on her cheek and everything. She raised her arms in invitation. Contentment enveloped him like a favorite blanket as he eased into them.

"Why are you dressed?" she murmured sleepily.

Not one to resist temptation, Zack shucked his shirt faster than Superman could change into his spandex. "Lady, you don't have to ask me twice."

Making love was fantastic, but there was also something comforting about snuggling. He was rubbing Liza's back and thinking it was time to get off the fence and lay his heart out. But then he remembered Angela. Before Zack proposed marriage—which he fully intended to do—he had to make sure his ex didn't mess things up.

THEY WERE PREPARING a late brunch when Zack told Liza about his two surprise phone calls. "What do you think they want?"

Liza shrugged as she took a carton of eggs out of the refrigerator. "I don't know. Do you feel like an omelet?"

"Sounds good."

Liza whisked the eggs so they were fluffy. "I imagine Helen's keeping it quiet because we're not exactly popular around the courthouse." She put a pat of butter in the skillet. "It's kind of strange, though. There won't be anyone around after five. The janitors don't start work until nine. You should take my bodyguard."

"Absolutely not. He's stays with you. I can take care of myself. I promise I'll be home by eight."

Still, there was something that felt off-kilter. "I'd really like to go with you," Liza said.

"No, that's not necessary. We'll go out to dinner after I get back, someplace romantic with candles and flowers."

Against her better judgment, she acquiesced. "Okay, but you be careful, now, ya hear."

"Yes, ma'am."

Chapter Thirty-Seven

Later that afternoon, Liza decided to pay her sister a visit. "Where's Zack?" Maizie asked as she snapped a hot-pink cape around Sue Lynn Throckmorton's broad shoulders. Liza lounged on the Victorian fainting couch, waiting for her sister to complete a makeover.

"He has a meeting at the courthouse. When he gets finished he's taking me out for a fancy dinner. I suppose that means I need to get dressed up. Wonder what he's planning?"

"That's my kind of a date." Maizie slathered white cream on her customer's face. "Sue Lynn, honey, I'm gonna make you beautiful. You just wait and see."

Frankly, Liza thought that would take a miracle. Sue Lynn Throckmorton was not just unattractive; she was clock-stoppingly ugly. However, she was heir apparent to Laverne Hightower. Which gave Liza an idea.

"Sue Lynn, you know Helen Damon, don't you?"

"Sure. I've known her since she moved here. Why?"

Liza shrugged. "We're working on a business deal and we could use her help. I don't know much about her other than her position on the board of supervisors."

Sue Lynn twirled around in the chair, thwarting Maizie's attempts to roll her hair. "I've heard that she and her brother were filthy rich. Their grandmama left them a trust fund, ya know. That's why I think she turned out so peculiar."

"Peculiar? What do you mean?"

Sue Lynn pursed her lips. "Now, this is just rumor, but I do know someone in Atlanta who graduated from high school with her. She said that Helen went to California after they graduated and got involved with some hippies." She leaned forward. "Haight-Ashbury. Drugs and stuff like that. After her brother was killed, she came back home."

It was the second time someone had mentioned Helen's brother. "They were twins, right?"

"Yes, indeedy. I hear they were thick as thieves." Sue Lynn cocked her head. "It was years ago, you know. But my friend said he was a strange duck, too. One night, he and a couple of buddies cut a fence at the construction site for that retirement village, Sunset Villas. Word is that they were planning to sabotage the heavy equipment, but he fell off one of the dozers. His buddies ran away and left him to die. Poor Helen never recovered, and now she lives by herself in that big old house she inherited from her grandmama."

It took a few moments for the implications to sink in.

Rob and Charlie's first big development job was the Sunset Villas. And Chris Carter and Bill Payton had also been involved.

No way—Helen couldn't be the murderer, could she? Liza felt she was finally putting the puzzle together. Helen was trying to avenge a long-dead brother. And she was hiding her true agenda behind an environmental facade. Grief could make people do incredibly stupid things.

"Are you absolutely positive about all this?" she demanded.

Sue Lynn nodded. "Uh-huh. Sure am."

Crap! Zack had already left to meet Helen. And his cell phone was at the office charging. Liza jumped up, looking for her bodyguard. "Where's Rocco?"

"I sent him to the bakery for coffee." Maizie reached for her hand. "What's wrong, honey?"

Liza grabbed her purse. "Helen might be the murderer, and

I'm afraid Zack's her next victim." She was trying, unsuccess-
fully, to keep the panic out of her voice. "I'm going to the courthouse. Call the bakery and tell Rocco to get over there
immediately. And phone Uncle Dave. Tell him what I just told
you." If she was overreacting, she'd worry about it later.

Maizie dropped the blow-dryer and grabbed her cell. "You're not
goin' anywhere without me." She beat Liza to the door. "Sue Lynn,
honey, lock up the shop for me. I'll do a complimentary later."

The twins jumped into Liza's car. Gravel spewed in every direction as they peeled out of the parking lot. In the meantime,
Maizie started making calls. Rocco said he was on his way. His
warning not to do anything until he got there fell on deaf ears.
The sheriff's office was another story. The 911 operator didn't
get too excited about the situation, so Maizie hung up on her and
called Uncle Dave at home.

"Uncle Dave, this is Maizie." She was one step away from
hysteria.

"Hey, kiddo. What's wrong?"

"Helen Damon's been behind this craziness all along and
now she's alone with Zack. You need to get to the courthouse—
we'll meet you there."

Uncle Dave didn't ask for more explanation. "I'm on my way.
Don't. Do. Anything!"

ZACK PARKED IN THE courthouse's deserted lot and went in search
of the door Helen had said would be unlocked. Bingo! He opened
it and found himself in a maze of small rooms and musty halls.
Document boxes were stacked everywhere and old furniture was
piled precariously. After taking a few wrong turns, he finally
found the elevator.

His footsteps echoed eerily on the stone floor of the empty
office building. In keeping with the architecture of the building,
the name of each occupant was lettered in elegant gold-leaf script
on the frosted-glass office doors. He tapped lightly on the door

labeled as Helen's and entered when he heard her lilting voice inviting him in.

Wearing a flowing caftan and her trademark Birkenstocks, Helen strolled around the desk to shake his hand.

She indicated the couch. "Please sit down. I've made some herbal tea. I also have some homemade banana-chocolate-chip muffins."

Helen ensconced herself in the chair opposite the couch.

"I asked you here to discuss the Bambi episode. It's deplorable. After your last meeting, Gaylon gave us a reluctant briefing. He must have been afraid we'd hear it somewhere else. In this town, that's a distinct possibility."

She reached for a mug on the end table and stared at the contents. "I've never trusted Gaylon. He's too slimy for my taste. That's why I decided to talk to you privately. But first, let's have a cup of tea."

Helen reached for a cozy covering a large teapot. She filled a mug and handed it to Zack. "It's my own mixture. I believe I told you I have a garden and an orchard."

She looked almost sad as she studied her own cup, then waved a hand in the air as if to dispel a troubling scene. "And please have a muffin. They're quite good. I use only organic ingredients."

Zack sipped the hot tea, bit into a muffin and half listened to her rambling monologue about crystals and massage therapy. He was pulled out of his daze when Helen flew to a bookcase across the room. She riffled through a stack of papers and returned with several folders that she tossed on the coffee table.

"I've heard rumors about Bambi over the years. So I made a point of doing a little research."

That got his attention.

"More tea?" Helen picked up the pot. "Surely you want a little more before we get down to business." She filled his cup before he had a chance to reply.

"And, my dear, you must have another sweet." She placed a

pastry on his plate. With her hostess duties attended to, Helen sat down and picked up one of the sheets of paper.

Everything was getting fuzzy. Zack felt as if he were watching an underwater movie. Presumably Helen was reading excerpts from a letter, but her speech seemed slurred and disjointed. He couldn't delineate what was real and what was hallucination.

His fight-or-flight reaction kicked in as he realized he was in a boatload of trouble. He'd let down his guard, and the oversight was going to get him killed. Zack slumped against the back of the couch, covering his eyes with his hand.

"Why?" he croaked.

"Why, my dear? You're about to find out what happens to people who try to destroy my little corner of the world. Developers killed my brother. They should have made sure no one could get into the construction site. And then they refused to take responsibility. So, I showed them. They paid with their lives. Rob Henderson cheated me by dying, and Charlie Taylor thinks he can get away from me. He won't, believe me. I'll get him."

She was baring her teeth in a semblance of a smile.

Zack didn't have a clue what she was talking about, but that no longer mattered. His last rational thought was that he'd seen the face of madness.

Chapter Thirty-Eight

Helen walked around the coffee table, staring with scorn at the unconscious man slumped on the couch. People were fools. It had been almost too easy to get the best of this one. Although he hadn't been on her original list, he was involved with the Blackwater Lake project. And speaking of imbeciles, she'd better let her cousins know they were needed.

"I've done my job and now it's your turn." Helen stepped aside as her coconspirators, Harvey and Tommy Ray, fell out of the closet. Blood was thicker than water and the two nitwits were Helen's second cousins twice removed. Add the fact that she knew all about their marijuana-smuggling operation and they were hers to control.

Harvey handcuffed Zack's hands and secured his feet with duct tape while Helen retrieved a pushcart from the next room.

"He's quite heavy, so I borrowed this from the janitor's closet. There shouldn't be anyone else in the building, but we still have to be careful. As soon as you leave, I'm going to have dinner with Alana Chen," she said. "It's a perfect alibi—don't you agree?" With that, she left her relatives to clean up the crime scene.

As Liza and Maizie skidded into the parking lot, a white van exited with its lights off.

"Damn! That has to be them. Hang on." Liza whipped the car around, taking off after the rapidly disappearing van.

A MAN IN A BEIGE HONDA WATCHED the activity with interest. When Rocco roared up, the man rolled down his window and yelled, "Get in. Looks like our client's been kidnapped. And his cute little girlfriend is in hot pursuit." He grinned at the look on the bodyguard's face.

"Here." He flipped open his wallet. "I'm a private investigator. Now get in, or we'll lose them."

Rocco was half out of his car before the man finished his sentence.

"I'm Atkins." The man tossed him a cell phone. "It's a full-size Econovan and I have a partial plate, HDL92-something. I didn't catch the rest of the numbers." He'd exited the parking lot before Rocco could finish punching in 911.

ZACK GRADUALLY BECAME AWARE of an ache that was threatening to pound through his forehead. He couldn't remember much, but whatever had happened, it packed a punch worthy of a margarita binge. He ran his tongue around his teeth. His mouth tasted as if a thousand camels had done their business in it.

Why couldn't he concentrate? And what was making his arms hurt?

Whack! He slid across the floor, colliding with a hard surface. His head was about to explode. He must have been drugged.

He couldn't see much in the darkness, but two things were starkly evident. First, he was trussed up like a Thanksgiving turkey; second, he was in the back of a moving vehicle with a maniac at the wheel.

It was obviously a utility van—no windows, no seats and no frills. The only light came from the cab where the driver and a passenger were engaged in a heated argument.

Zack made a quick inventory of his situation. They thought he was unconscious. That was good. And he could feel the small Swiss Army knife in his pocket. That was fantastic! The nincompoops hadn't done a very thorough job frisking him, but no one ever said crooks were smart. Very quietly, Zack managed to retrieve the knife from his pocket. Getting it open was another story, but when he'd accomplished that task, he took a few deep breaths to slow his heartbeat, and then started to work on the tape around his ankles. Not an easy job when his hands were cuffed in back, especially considering the way his thighs were cramping.

The people in the front seat continued their argument, but the road noise made it impossible for Zack to hear more than snippets of the conversation. Several references were made to the recent kidnappings. He couldn't believe he'd been conned by a middle-aged hippie.

Enough of the Monday-morning quarterbacking. Survival would take luck and cunning. Zack ignored his painful muscles as he attempted to get his hands repositioned in front. But, try as he might, he couldn't pull that one off. Jeez, that hurt! If he managed to get out of this mess, he swore he'd stretch every day.

From the van's speed, he presumed they were on a highway. It was probably a safe bet they were headed to the lake. What better place to get rid of a body? The driver turned off the main road and made a sharp turn onto a gravel lane.

Zack finally managed to get his feet free. Now he had to come up with a plan. If he didn't, he was a dead man.

"HE EXITED ON SWAMP CREEK ROAD," Maizie screeched, clinging to the armrest. "Hurry, hurry!"

Not Swamp Creek Road! There were so many little crossroads that if they lost sight of the van, it could take hours to find it again.

"Keep your eyes on those taillights and tell me if they disappear."

Maizie squealed when they hit a huge rut.

ROCCO AND ATKINS FOLLOWED Liza's car until it turned onto the gravel road. Atkins went several hundred feet past the lane before pulling off.

"I'm going to back up and follow them with my lights off. I'm afraid Ms. Henderson is going to get in real trouble by running in there. Call the locals again and tell them where we are. The sign we just passed said Swamp Creek Road. My guess is that the deputies aren't far behind us."

THE PINGING OF GRAVEL AGAINST the undercarriage gradually yielded to a series of teeth-jarring jolts. When the van came to a stop, the silence was almost overwhelming. Zack heard another car door slam, and the van's driver and passenger jumped out. That meant there were at least three people who wanted him dead.

Zack lay motionless, listening intently as the door of the van slid open. He was outnumbered, but he had surprise on his side. A tall man leaned into the van, giving Zack the perfect opportunity to land a vicious kick to guy's family jewels.

The man howled in pain, stumbling back into his companions. Zack rolled out of the van, lunging toward the sanctuary of the woods.

The other man hollered. "Get him, stupid. Shoot him! Give me the gun."

Zack charged through the undergrowth, unaware of the branches slapping his body as he ran. He tripped over a log and fell face-first into the water. Picking himself up, he quickly took stock of his situation. He'd been following the lakeshore. Maybe he could turn that into an advantage—he wasn't sure how, but he was willing to give it a try. In the distance he could hear shouts and more gunfire.

He crept behind an ancient oak, taking a moment to catch his breath. The darkness of the forest was broken only by a light flickering in the distance.

Damn! His stalkers had flashlights, and they weren't far away. Zack could hear voices reverberating through the trees. Strangely enough it sounded as if they were calling his name.

When he glanced over his shoulder to see how far back his

pursuers were, he failed to notice a tree root. One minute he was running; the next second he was flying through the air. Considering his luck, he'd probably land in a nest of water moccasins.

Chapter Thirty-Nine

The first thing Liza saw when she drove into the clearing was Zack running into the forest. One man was sprawled on the ground holding his crotch while another scampered toward the trees. The scene would have been comical if it hadn't been so deadly. Liza didn't recognize them, but she realized they were the killers.

"You don't have a weapon in your purse, do you?" Liza asked.

Maizie gave her one of her better "duh" looks. "Are you nuts?"

"Then we'll have to use the car. I hope my insurance covers this." Actually, she didn't much care.

"Go for it." Maizie clutched the armrest so tightly her knuckles were white.

Liza aimed her vehicle at the van. At the last second she swerved to minimize the crash. What she wouldn't give for a 9mm Glock. A pair of nail clippers and a paring knife weren't going to be very effective. The most she could hope for was a diversion, giving Zack a chance to escape.

After the collision, Liza and Maizie tumbled out of the car, hunkering down behind the rear wheel.

"Okay, Nancy Drew. Now what?" Maizie whispered.

"I'm thinking, I'm thinking." Liza was thinking she was about to get them both killed. "You go into the woods."

"No way!" A shot pinged off the hood of the car, putting an end to their bickering.

A beige Honda skidded to a stop and two men rolled out, guns drawn. It was Rocco and a friend.

The guys in the clearing stared bug-eyed at the newcomers. Although one man continued to cup his privates, the other threw his hands in the air.

"Drop the gun," Rocco roared, "Now!"

"Me?" The second man looked up, apparently amazed that he was holding a pistol.

"Yeah, dummy, you."

When he threw it at Rocco's feet, it discharged.

"Watch out! You're gonna kill someone." Oh yeah, he already had.

A patrol car raced into the clearing. Rocco, in an act of self-preservation, raised his hands and faced the policemen. One deputy retrieved the weapons while the other guarded the people lying facedown.

Liza clutched the policeman. "Stumpy, Zack's out there. You have to help him."

WHEN THE SEARCH AND RESCUE folks found Zack, he was muddy and bruised, but unbroken. Reminders of the debacle included a wide range of scratches, abrasions and insect bites which were currently being treated in the emergency room.

Liza hovered over him like a mother hen after the doctor left them alone in the curtained area.

"Are you okay?"

"Just a little dizzy, but other than that, I'm fine," Zack said, rubbing the bridge of his nose.

"I thought they were going to kill you."

He grimaced as he flexed his hands. "I wasn't terribly optimistic myself. I figured I had about a twenty percent shot of getting out of there." He grinned and flashed her his dimples. "But I didn't know you were coming to my rescue."

She couldn't wait a minute longer to hug him. When she grabbed him, Zack groaned. "Does that hurt?"

"Only when I breathe. I strained my back while I was trying to cut the tape on my ankles. Either then or when I fell into the water." He displayed another dimple. "I suppose I need to get to the gym more often."

"Uncle Dave wants to talk to you. He has the district attorney with him. I told him he had to wait."

"You're one of the only people who could get away with that." Liza suspected he was right.

The young E.R. doc pushed the curtain aside. "You're good to go. Take these for pain if you need them." He handed Zack a bottle of pills. Liza stepped out into the hall to speak to her uncle.

"He'll be here in a minute, Uncle Dave." She kissed his cheek. "I'm going to the cafeteria while you guys chat," she said before strolling down the corridor.

SHERIFF MADISON was leaning against the wall when Zack emerged. "Liza said you want to talk to me."

"Yep, we sure do," Dave said with a smile. "Let's go in there and sit down." He indicated a small conference room. "I'm sure you're feeling pretty sore, and if I don't take care of you, Liza will have my hide.

"I'd like you to meet Rick Hall, our district attorney. This isn't going to take long, is it, Rick?" Dave gave the lawyer a good-natured poke in the ribs.

"Nope. I'll keep it brief. But there are a couple of items we need to discuss."

Zack was used to the drill. "Let's do it."

"How much do you know about the murders?"

"Enough, I suppose. They're the reason Charlie Taylor left town. But what I don't understand is why someone would want to harm me."

"Helen hasn't said a word. She lawyered up, but Harvey Spellman, her cousin, has been singing like an Irish tenor. According to him, Helen was furious about your Blackwater Lake development project. Originally she was going after Charlie and his friends. But somewhere along the way she decided to also get rid of you and Liza. And considering the leverage Helen had on her cousins, they didn't have much choice but to play along. For a bunch of morons, they were remarkably successful."

"We couldn't seem to stop them." Dave scratched his head. "Actually, I think they were too stupid to get caught."

Rick nodded in agreement.

"Anyway, we'll need you to stick around to testify. Will that be a problem?" Sheriff Dave asked.

Zack wondered whether he was asking as a lawman or a concerned relative. "No, I have no intention of leaving. I do have a question, though. One of the security people was working for me, but how does the other guy fit in?"

"You didn't hear? Your ex-wife hired him to keep an eye on you and, um, Mrs. Henderson," Rick Hall answered. "He's been following you for almost a month. Fortunately for us, and for you, both of them were armed. But, I have to give it to Mrs. Henderson and her sister. They were damn brave."

"Liza and Maizie are something else, aren't they?"

Sheriff Dave grinned. "Yep. It runs in the family."

Zack thought about Angela. She'd hired a man to follow him. No doubt about it—she was a certifiably psychotic. As much as Zack hated to do it, he had to return to San Francisco and have it out with her, once and for all.

Chapter Forty

After they finished with the police and the emergency room, Zack and Liza went back to Belle Meade.

She left him to sit at on the veranda while she made iced tea. This was the crucial moment. Now that the crisis was over, would he stay in Magnolia Bluffs or scoot off to California? She'd bet her bottom dollar he was history.

Sure, they'd had some lusty moments, and for her it had grown into soul-deep love. But he hadn't once uttered the *L* word. Did he love her? Or was he too jaded to make a commitment?

Zack stretched out when she returned to the porch, trying to find a position that was comfortable. He patted the seat next to him. "Come sit with me."

Liza put the tray of tea and cookies on the table and cozied up beside him.

He played with her hair, then rubbed his hands up and down her arms. "We need to talk."

Those were four words no sane woman ever wanted to hear.

"I love you."

What! Her eyes popped open. "Say that again," she demanded.

"I love you."

"And…"

"And what?"

"And I hear a 'but' coming."

He wanted to pop the question, but he wanted to do it right. "I love you and we need to have a serious talk about where we're going from here. But first I have to go back to San Francisco to clear up some stuff with Angela. I'm leaving tomorrow."

Unfortunately, she didn't give him a chance to say that he was planning to move to Magnolia Bluffs.

"What!" Liza jumped up and glared at him, hands on her hips. "Just like a man. Say 'I love you,' and in the next breath, 'I'm leaving.' Let me tell you something, buddy boy." She got in his face, poking him in the chest. "That's not gonna hack it with me."

He had the terrible urge to grin, but the murderous look on her face forced him to bite it back.

Waiting to buy a ring had been a strategic error, but Zack was determined. "I won't be there long. Like I said, I'm making a quick trip to San Francisco. I'll be back before you know it." He started to explain about his crazy ex-wife, but Liza interrupted him again.

"Yeah, yeah, whatever." She brushed him aside and stomped inside.

Zack wondered what she was doing. The banging sounds were not encouraging. He soon had his answer. His black duffel bag landed on the floor by his feet.

"All things considered, I think you should recuperate at a hotel. I'll drive you over and make sure you have a ride to the airport."

Zack nodded. He knew exactly what his intentions were. But with the snit she was in, he was better off keeping his mouth shut—at least for now.

EVEN THOUGH THE HOTEL was the plushest in town, the bed was hard and the pillows felt like bricks. Zack missed Liza's big four-poster bed, and he especially missed having her snuggled up next to him. But his first priority had to be dealing with Angela. He picked up the phone to call his ex-wife, determined to be firm and reasonable.

"Angela, this is Zack."

"Why, hello, darling."

"Don't 'darling' me. Tell me why you hired a detective to follow me." So much for keeping his cool.

"I want to save our marriage, and to do that I had to find out what you were doing in Georgia. It wasn't easy to even discover where you were."

"Angela, we will *never* be married again. You have to stop fantasizing." His comment started the waterworks, but Zack ignored her hysterics. Tears no longer affected him. "When I get back to San Francisco we'll settle this permanently, even if I have to obtain a restraining order."

LIZA WAS ON THE FAINTING couch in Maizie's boutique holding a pint of double-fudge-brownie ice cream in one hand and an Oreo cookie in the other. Maizie had taken one look at her sister's face, closed the shop and pulled out the chocolate arsenal.

"Tell me all about it."

"He said he loved me, and in the next breath he told me he was going back to San Francisco," Liza wailed. "I knew I'd get my heart broken. You spouted all that nonsense about hot sex and letting things run their course. Let me tell you, big sister, this hurts like nobody's business." She punctuated her assertion with a sob.

Maizie disappeared into the back room and returned with another pint of ice cream.

"Did you tell him you loved him?"

Liza licked her spoon. "Nope."

"And did he say he wasn't ever coming back?"

"No. He said he'd be back soon."

Maizie lifted her shoulders. "I rest my case. You need to get a grip. Then talk to the boy. You're both doofuses."

"I'm not a doofus," Liza muttered, and then giggled. "Well, maybe a little one. So what should I do?"

"Call the hotel and make sure he's still there. Then go over and have it out with him."

She needed to work up the courage.

Maizie threw the cell phone into her lap. "Do it! Right now!"

Liza reluctantly punched in the number.

"What do you mean he's checked out?" she asked the clerk who answered.

"Madam, I mean Mr. Maynard has paid his bill and left."

"No," she howled.

"Yes." The hotel clerk terminated the connection—not that Liza could blame him. He had a crazy woman on the line.

She had to get to the airport—immediately. Without even saying goodbye, Liza ran out and jumped into her car. Stupid! Stupid! Stupid! She hadn't asked the clerk what time he'd checked out. For all she knew he was already halfway to the West Coast. But she was determined to talk to him, and that meant a record-breaking trip to Hartsfield.

An hour later Liza was sprinting to the terminal. Where was Mr. Tall, Dark and Handsome?

Thank the Lord—there he was in all his sinfully sexy glory. Liza bypassed the line and came sliding up just as Zack reached the check-in counter. She grabbed the handle of his suitcase when he tried to put it on the scale. "You can't go."

When he grinned, his dimples were as deep as the Grand Canyon. "And why not?"

"Because." That was as much of an answer as she could manage.

"Sir, are you still going?" the clerk asked.

Zack and Liza answered simultaneously.

"Yes."

"No."

Zack held Liza close. "Let me get my ticket. I won't be gone long."

"Sir, if you want to make your flight, we need to get you checked in."

"Sure." Zack shoved his ID across the counter.

"You have twenty minutes before they close the doors," the

woman said, handing him his boarding pass. "I'd hurry if I were you."

Zack took Liza's arm, pulling her with him toward the security line. Then, right there in front of God and the TSA folks, Zack kissed her until she saw stars.

"You crack me up." He kissed her again. "Just remember the immortal words of General MacArthur—I shall return. I love you like crazy. You're going to be stuck with me for at least the next fifty years. And while I'm in California I plan to buy you the biggest diamond I can find. As soon as I get back, I'm plunking it on your finger. Count on it. Now, don't get into any trouble while I'm gone. Remember, I love you."

With those words, he passed through security and took off at a dead run.

Epilogue

Kansas—one year later

Zack's hands were white-knuckled on the steering wheel. "We're in a lot of trouble." They'd been visiting his mom and were on their way back to the airport.

No kidding! Armageddon was racing across the prairie in a boiling cauldron of black clouds. Rain was pounding down, and the wind had kicked up, sending debris tumbling across the road. Liza had seen storms in Georgia, but this was beyond anything she'd ever experienced. When a bolt of lightning hit a nearby telephone pole, the hair on her arms came to attention.

"Will we get a tornado?" She tried to keep the panic out of her voice but she squeaked on the last syllable.

Zack gave her a look she couldn't decipher. "Check the map and see how far we are from the next town." He was fighting to keep the car on the road. "We have to find some shelter."

She was rummaging through the console when something big smashed against the windshield. Her first impulse was to scream, but instead she decided to go for levity. "Was that Toto?"

Her joke fell flat. "It was hail, and we're about to get pummeled."

Day turned to night, and Liza muttered every prayer she'd ever heard as ice balls devastated the SUV. Whether God could hear her over the cacophony was anyone's guess.

Liza scrunched down in the seat, distracting herself by reflecting on the events of the past year. True to his word, Zack had returned from San Francisco with a ring in his pocket. It had taken nearly six months to take care of the logistics related to Rob's estate. But once those had been settled, she'd felt free to say yes and plan a wedding.

So with the entire family—his and hers—in attendance, they were married on Halloween. And no, she hadn't decorated with orange and black, but they had served chocolate cake and trick-or-treat candy.

Uncle Dave had been delighted when Zack had asked for a job. He was well-known in town thanks to his involvement in solving the murders. In fact, Uncle Dave was now thinking about retirement and making plans to help Zack run for sheriff. Life was sweet. The Blackwater Lake project had even skated through with the help of G. Harry. Would wonders neve cease?

But right this minute, she was afraid she was about to see Dorothy fly by.

"Tornadoes come from the south." The tension in Zack's voice was almost enough to send her over the edge.

"Which way's south?" she yelped.

"That way." He indicated the passenger-side window.

Liza got brave and took a peek. "Is that what I think it is?"

"Yeah. We're almost to town."

Although it was virtually impossible to see through the torrential rain, she spotted a grain silo and a couple of buildings.

"We're going to take shelter at the first place we find. When I stop the car, you get out and run inside. Get under a table, a bar, whatever you can find."

"You'll be right behind me, won't you?"

"Get ready." He skidded to a halt in front of a diner. "Jump and run! Now!"

Liza was barely out of the car before Zack caught up to her. Thank God the door to the restaurant was unlocked.

"Run toward the kitchen—they're bound to have a walk-in freezer!" he screamed. When the front window blew out, it felt as if all the air was being sucked out of the building.

"There!" Zack pushed her toward their only hope of safety. He jerked the steel door open and shoved her along.

"Get in!" Someone was already there. In fact, when she looked around, Liza realized the freezer was full of people. Several men shouldered their way through the crowd to help Zack close the door. Then everyone squatted down, listening to the freight train roar over. There was a huge crash and the entire building shuddered.

"That was the roof," Zack said. Even though he was practically lying on top of her, she could barely hear him above the racket.

And then there was blessed silence, punctuated only by soft sobs and expletives.

"Is it over?" Liza asked.

"I think so, but we'd better wait for a bit."

Five minutes later one of the men opened the door, only to find rain pouring down. It looked as if a giant had ripped off the roof and scooped out the contents of the building.

"Do you think anyone needs help?" The cop in Zack always came out in an emergency.

"No, son." A man in a white apron clapped him on the back. "The whole town is here. We always joked that the freezer would be our storm cellar. I guess it came in handy this time."

Liza tried to stand, but her legs were rubbery. "Take a look and see if the car's gone."

Zack stuck his head out the door. "I don't see it. The rental folks aren't going to be happy."

"I know, but that's okay. We're alive and safe, that's what's important." Then and there, Liza realized how precious and short life could be, and she planned to live it to the fullest.

"I love you." She kissed him until his toes curled. "One thing's for sure—our life will never be boring."

* * * * *

Enjoy a sneak preview of
MATCHMAKING WITH A MISSION
by B.J. Daniels,
part of the WHITEHORSE, MONTANA *miniseries.*
Available from Harlequin Intrigue
in April 2008.

Nate Dempsey has returned to Whitehorse to uncover the truth about his past…

Nate sensed someone watching the house and looked out in surprise to see a woman astride a paint horse just on the other side of the fence. He quickly stepped back from the filthy second-floor window, although he doubted she could have seen him. Only a little of the June sun pierced the dirty glass to glow on the dust-coated floor at his feet as he waited a few heartbeats before he looked out again.

The place was so isolated he hadn't expected to see another soul. Like the front yard, the dirt road was waist-high with weeds. When he'd broken the lock on the back door, he'd had to kick aside a pile of rotten leaves that had blown in from last fall.

As he sneaked a look, he saw that she was still there, staring at the house in a way that unnerved him. He shielded his eyes from the glare of the sun off the dirty window and studied her, taking in her head of long blond hair that feathered out in the breeze from under her Western straw hat.

She wore a tan canvas jacket, jeans and boots. But it was the way she sat astride the brown-and-white horse that nudged the memory.

He felt a chill as he realized he'd seen her before. In that very spot. She'd been just a kid then. A kid on a pretty paint horse. Not this one—the markings were different. Anyway, it couldn't have been the same horse, considering the last time he had seen her was more than twenty years ago. That horse would be dead by now.

His mind argued it probably wasn't even the same girl. But he knew better. It was the way she sat on the horse, so at home in a saddle and secure in her world on the other side of that fence.

To the boy he'd been, she and her horse had represented freedom, a freedom he'd known he would never have—even after he escaped this house.

Nate saw her shift in the saddle, and for a moment he feared she planned to dismount and come toward the house. With Ellis Harper in his grave, there would be little to keep her away.

To his relief, she reined her horse around and rode back the way she'd come.

As he watched her ride away, he thought about the way she'd stared at the house—today and years ago. While the smartest thing she could do was to stay clear of this house, he had a feeling she'd be back.

Finding out her name should prove easy, since he figured she must live close by. As for her interest in Harper House... He would just have to make sure it didn't become a problem.

* * * * *

Be sure to look for
MATCHMAKING WITH A MISSION
and other suspenseful Harlequin Intrigue stories,
available in April
wherever books are sold.

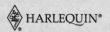

HARLEQUIN® Romance®

presents

The Wedding Planners

Planning perfect weddings... finding happy endings!

Amidst the rustle of satins and silks, the scent of red roses and white lilies and the excited chatter of brides-to-be, six friends from Boston are The Wedding Belles—they make other people's wedding dreams come true....

But are they always the wedding planner...never the bride?

Who will be the next to say "I do"?

And don't miss the exciting wedding-planner tips and author reminiscences that accompany each book!

www.eHarlequin.com   HRI7507

REQUEST YOUR FREE BOOKS!

2 FREE NOVELS PLUS 2
FREE GIFTS!

Heart, Home & Happiness!

YES! Please send me 2 FREE Harlequin American Romance® novels and my 2 FREE gifts (gifts are worth about $10). After receiving them, if I don't wish to receive any more books, I can return the shipping statement marked "cancel." If I don't cancel, I will receive 4 brand-new novels every month and be billed just $4.24 per book in the U.S. or $4.99 per book in Canada, plus 25¢ shipping and handling per book and applicable taxes, if any*. That's a savings of close to 15% off the cover price! I understand that accepting the 2 free books and gifts places me under no obligation to buy anything. I can always return a shipment and cancel at any time. Even if I never buy another book from Harlequin, the two free books and gifts are mine to keep forever.

154 HDN EEZK   354 HDN EEZV

Name _____ (PLEASE PRINT) _____

Address _____ Apt. # _____

City _____ State/Prov. _____ Zip/Postal Code _____

Signature (if under 18, a parent or guardian must sign) _____

Mail to the **Harlequin Reader Service:**
IN U.S.A.: P.O. Box 1867, Buffalo, NY 14240-1867
IN CANADA: P.O. Box 609, Fort Erie, Ontario L2A 5X3

Not valid to current subscribers of Harlequin American Romance books.

Want to try two free books from another line?
Call 1-800-873-8635 or visit www.morefreebooks.com.

* Terms and prices subject to change without notice. N.Y. residents add applicable sales tax. Canadian residents will be charged applicable provincial taxes and GST. This offer is limited to one order per household. All orders subject to approval. Credit or debit balances in a customer's account(s) may be offset by any other outstanding balance owed by or to the customer. Please allow 4 to 6 weeks for delivery. Offer available while quantities last.

Your Privacy: Harlequin is committed to protecting your privacy. Our Privacy Policy is available online at www.eHarlequin.com or upon request from the Reader Service. From time to time we make our lists of customers available to reputable third parties who may have a product or service of interest to you. If you would prefer we not share your name and address, please check here. ☐

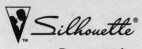

Silhouette®

Romantic
SUSPENSE

**Sparked by Danger,
Fueled by Passion.**

The Taken

Tierney Doyle is used to being criticized for
her psychic abilities, yet the tough-as-nails—
and drop-dead-gorgeous—detective has no doubt
about what she has uncovered in the case of a
string of unsolved murders. And Tierney is slowly
discovering that working so close to her partner,
detective Wade Callahan, could be lethal.

Look for

Danger Signals
by Kathleen Creighton

Available in April wherever books are sold.

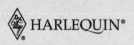
HARLEQUIN®

American ★ Romance®

COMING NEXT MONTH

#1205 RUNAWAY COWBOY by Judy Christenberry
The Lazy L Ranch
Jessica Ledbetter has worked too hard on her family's dude ranch to let
Jim Bradford, a cowboy turned power broker and the ranch's new manager,
show her up. The Lazy L is Jess's legacy, and she isn't about to let it fall into
the hands of an outsider. No matter what those hands can do to her...

#1206 MARRYING THE BOSS by Megan Kelly
When Mark Collins finds himself in a competition with Leanne Fairbanks for
the position of CEO of the family business, he can't believe it. But as they go
head-to-head in a series of tasks to fight for the top job, Mark begins to see her
as more than just a rival. And if he wins, will he lose *her?*

#1207 THE MARRIAGE RECIPE by Michele Dunaway
Catching her fiancé in bed with one of the restaurant's curvaceous employees
sends up-and-coming pastry chef Rachel Palladia fleeing Manhattan for the
comforts of home. But when her ex threatens to sue for her dessert recipes, she
turns to her high school heartthrob, Colin Morris, who happens to be the town
lawyer—and he's a lot sweeter than revenge!

#1208 DOWN HOME DIXIE by Pamela Browning
No real Southern belle would fall for a Yankee—especially not one named
Kyle Sherman. But Dixie Lee Smith does, and hides the truth about his
illustrious ancestor from her family. What's worse, as soon as she finds out
she's got competition, *she* goes to war—to keep the handsome Northerner
for herself!

www.eHarlequin.com

HARCNM0308